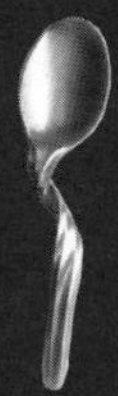

THE UNFINISHED LIFE OF PHOEBE HICKS

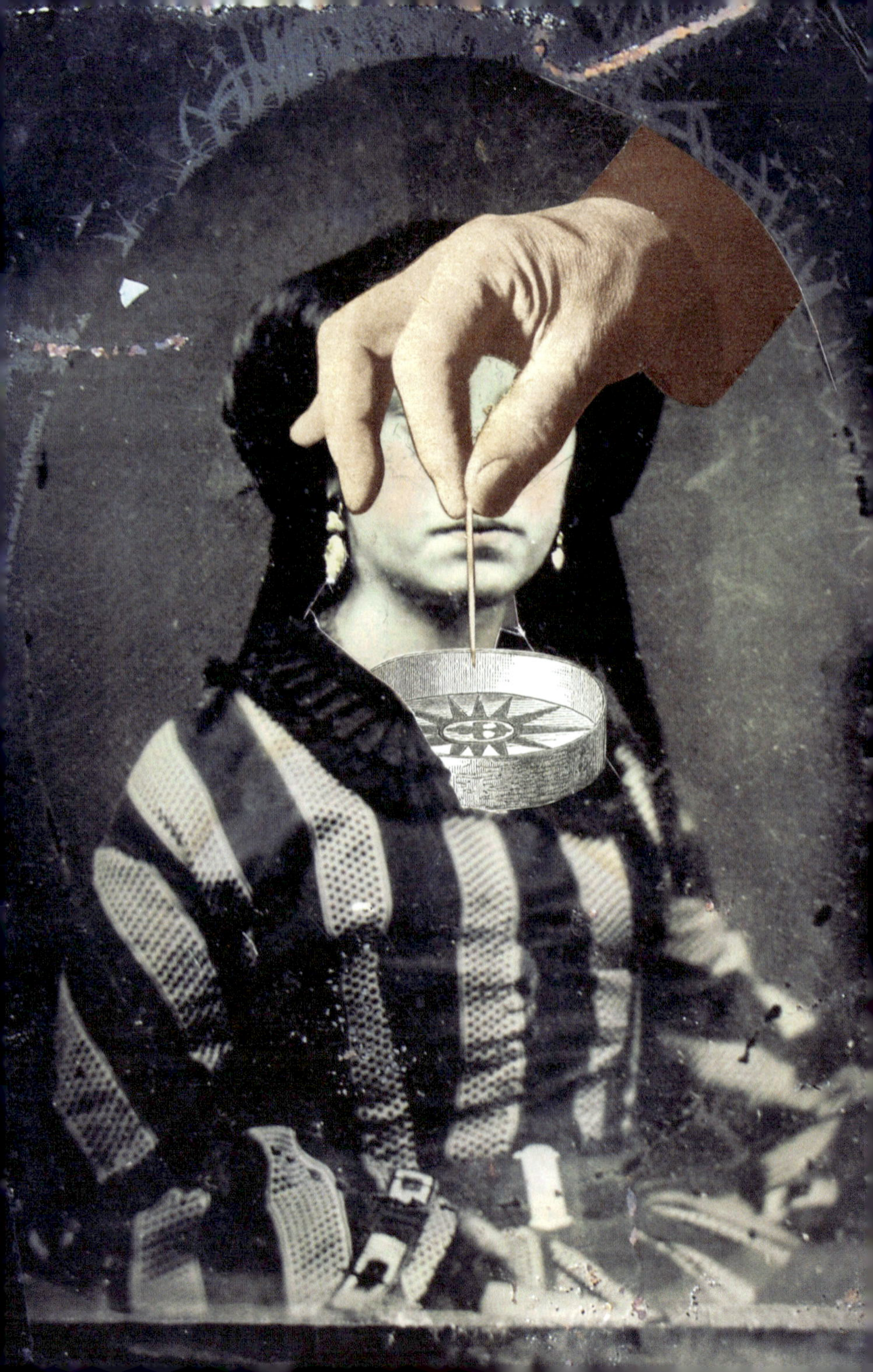

Agnieszka Taborska

THE UNFINISHED LIFE OF PHOEBE HICKS

Translated from the Polish by
URSULA PHILLIPS

Collages by
SELENA KIMBALL

TWISTED SPOON PRESS
PRAGUE
2024

ISBN 978-80-88628-01-9

This publication has been supported by the ©POLAND Translation Program

To the magic city of Providence

The Victorian period was not only a haunted age; it was also, in every sense of the word, a hallucinatory age, lending itself to every type of illusion, even at the level of bricks and mortar. The Victorian house, the Victorian street, encouraged illusion and hallucination, the Victorian theatre was a hotbed of optical tricks, only the kitchen escaped the obsession with the manufacture of articles which appeared to be something else: money-boxes disguised as books, substantial-looking doors that on examination was merely cunning paintwork, solid-looking chairs that were, in fact, featherlight, being manufactured from papier-mâché. Nineteenth-century man and woman were disposed to believe [. . .] that things were not as they seemed. Their senses had a habit of letting them down, and they were mentally prepared for any odd happenings, fugitive visions, the unaccountable thing seen out of the corner of the eye, the strange sounds in the middle of the night, the tap on the shoulder that might be a visitation from another world.

— Ronald Pearsall
The Table-Rappers: The Victorians and the Occult

NOSTALGIA

It was the year when a vague, indefinable restlessness seized the inhabitants of Providence and gnawed at their souls. They were plagued mid-century — as in the first half — by a damp and sweltering August. The mosquitoes, exceptionally annoying that summer, made the empty streets after sundown feel all the more deserted. Their high-pitched whine and the occasional distant wail of a child trapped in some baking room, reverberated in the air. The lucky few had left in time for the ocean : for Little Compton or the islands of Nantucket and Block Island. There the early mornings and evenings brought fresher gusts of wind and the fish lying on ice-covered tables in the harbour, caught only moments before, whetted something resembling an appetite. Yet even in Little Compton it was hard to walk down the cobbled streets in the middle of the day. There was nothing to do except sit on the shore in a wicker strand-chair with one's back to the sun and count on the barely perceptible sea-breeze, or seek in a darkened room answers to the same questions tormenting the inhabitants of Providence who had remained in town.

Like the rest of humanity, the citizens of Providence would have gladly devoted themselves to some useful occupation — the women happily spending sultry evenings crocheting doilies, the men proudly organizing hunting parties. That summer, however, even such simple pursuits filled them with nostalgia. After their death, what would become of the snow-white doilies painstakingly folded and stored in cavernous chests? Who would dust the antlers sticking out at such a curious angle over the fireplace?

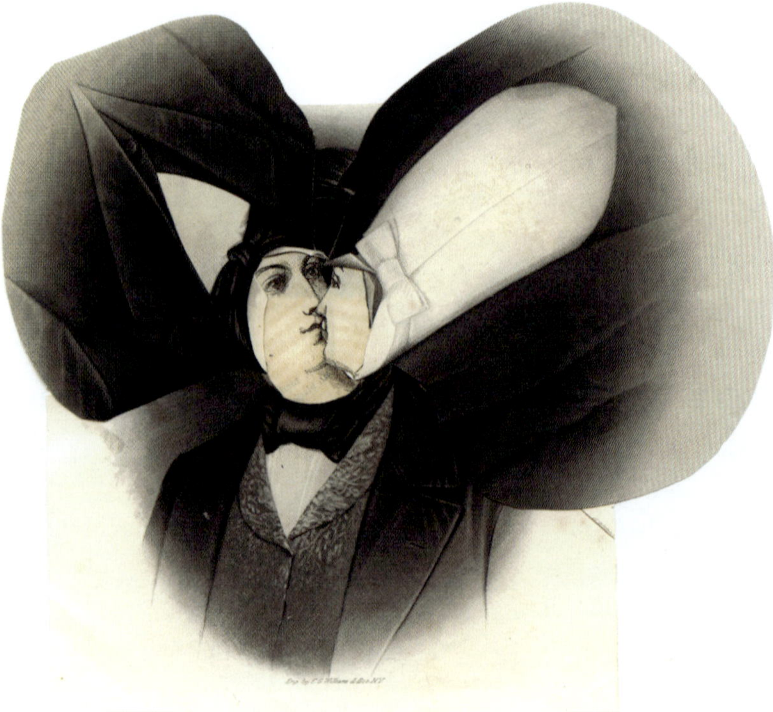

Such questions tormented the citizens of Providence, struggling in summer to catch their breath and strolling in autumn beneath the famous New England maples, whose colours changed through over thirty shades of scarlet and pink. Thank God the inhabitants of the harbour town didn't have to dwell on dismal thoughts in the long winter dragging on mercilessly from December to April. The problem resolved itself earlier : in November 1847.

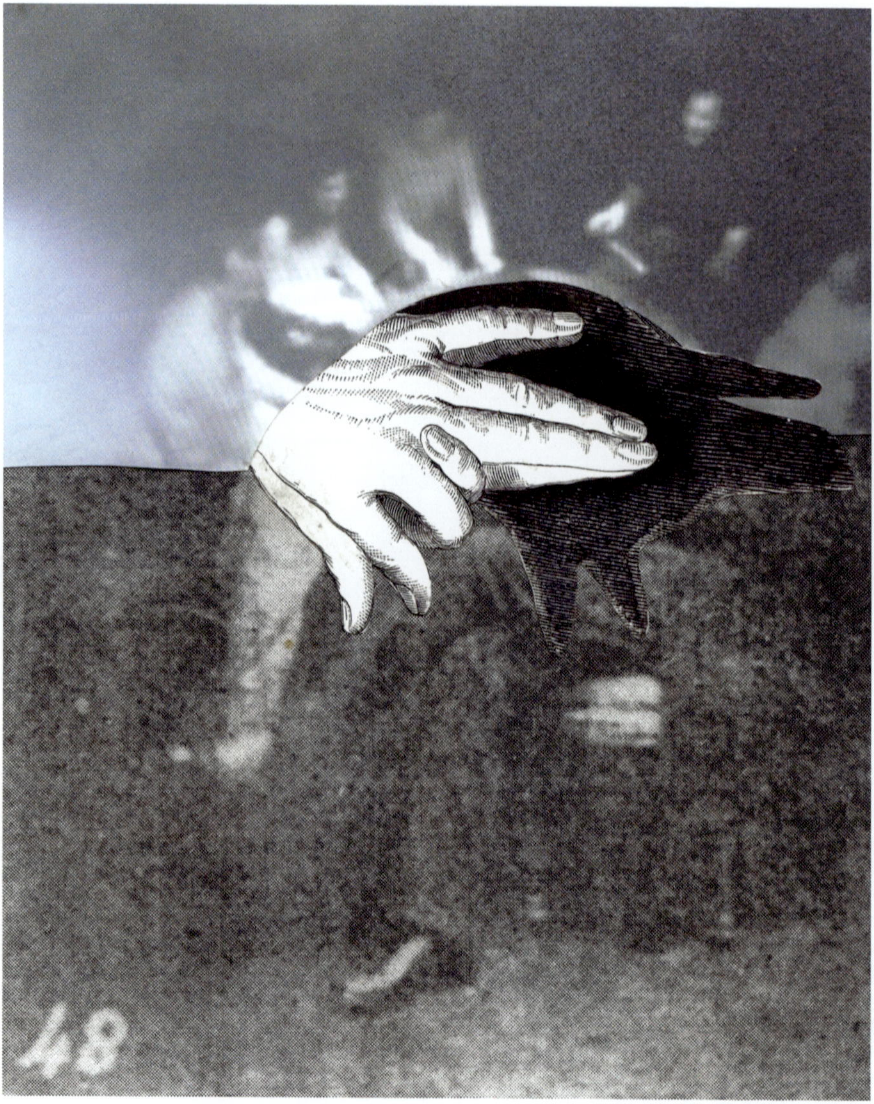
48

THE TIME WAS RIPE FOR SPIRITUALIST SÉANCES

Half a century meanwhile was passing into oblivion, bearing away with it long-haired heroines despairing on Romantic canvases. What its second half would bring remained an enigma to minds exhausted by a strange anxiety. At the end of October no one suspected the time was ripe for spiritualist séances.

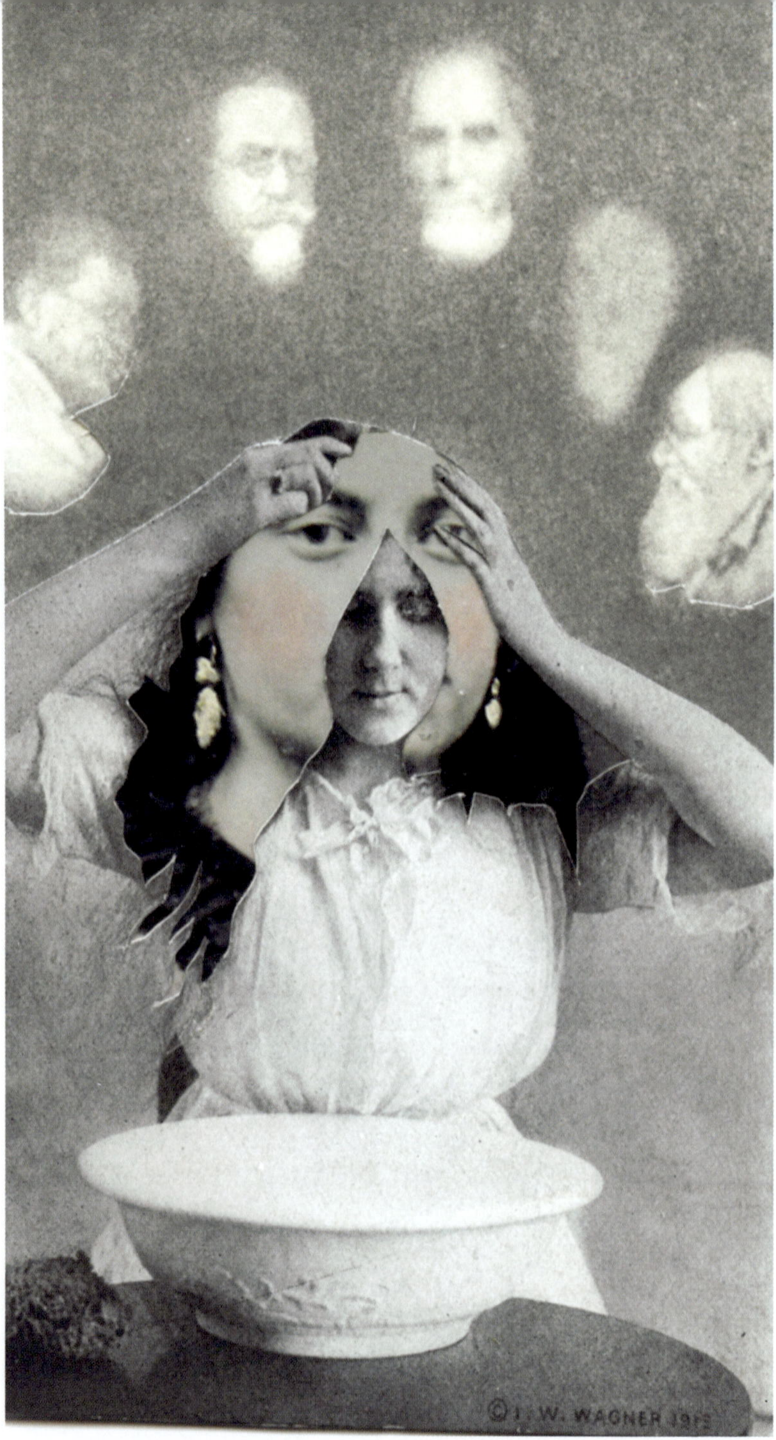
© I. W. WAGNER

CLAM FRITTERS

The theory that a piece of clam, which had found its way into a culinary delicacy known across New England, gave birth to spiritualist photography is no exaggeration. This toxic morsel was the very root of the madness possessing the hearts and minds of New England puritans for decades to come.

On 1 November 1847 Phoebe Hicks returned home earlier than usual. Barely over the threshold, she rushed into her bedroom, and instead of climbing onto the high and, by today's standards, rather short bed ran straight to the washstand. She leaned over and threw up — once, twice, unable to control herself, even after the third time. She vomited all night, occasionally rinsing her perspiring face in water from the blue-sprigged ewer. After only an hour, she had nothing left inside but brown bile, which she continued to bring up. Strands of black hair escaped from her tightly-wound bun — stiff, sticky, stinking — and clung to her cheeks like seaweed. She shivered all over — hands numb, head splitting from the violent convulsions. Her back ached, jammed like her knees in an awkward position. The skin over her entire body acquired an unpleasant hypersensitivity, reacting to the slightest imagined breath of air. Her corset, unlaced by the last remnants of strength, became an instrument of torture boring into the secret recesses of her body desperate for sleep. Shoes, suddenly tight, cut into her toes, her dress drenched in whatever had missed the overflowing basin. Every new paroxysm brought the wretched Phoebe to the verge of a faint. Many times in the night, the thought occurred she might not last until morning and would die in this non-aesthetic manner, the unexpected victim

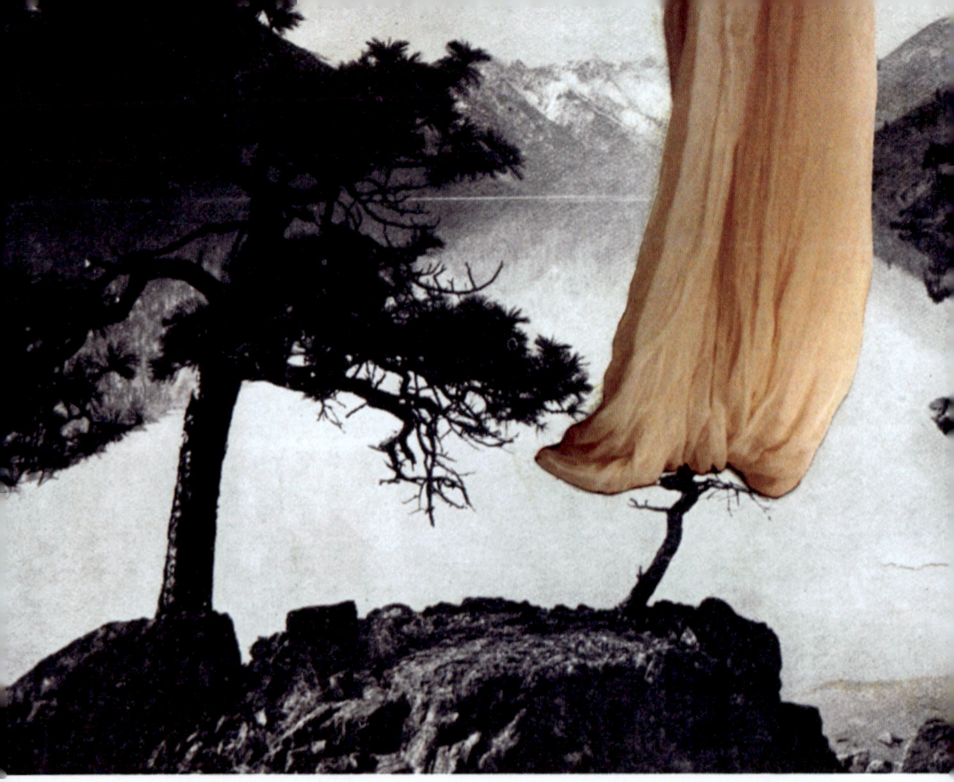

of clam fritters. Yet the prospect of death releasing her once and for all from any obligation to taste the fried fare was not entirely unwelcome — so dreadful was her memory of the restaurant serving the harbour specialty, furnished with its round tables covered in blue-check cloths.

Dusk reigned in the bedroom. Then darkness descended, until the sun rose again, casting its cold rays onto the washstand. The dawning of the new day was a slow and painful spectacle.

Phoebe's thoughts strayed throughout New England. They chose mid-summer, as if to spite the grey November twilight. Scurried along the widow's walks of brown houses, where fishermen's wives waited patiently for boats to return. Ran the length of white fences around the homes of judges and pastors.

Marvelled at rococo gates at odds with spartan façades. Rested in porches cluttered with wicker furniture. Breathed deeply over the bay and clung to the red brick of harbour buildings. Frowned at news of an approaching storm. Lapsed into a reverie over Providence, its existence forever bound to the ocean. Crashed into heights that gave the town its shape like the seven hills of Rome. Flew over the snow-white belfries of Baptist churches. Landed on windswept beaches and burrowed for fun in the sand. Scrambled over sharp rocks by the seashore, mussel-covered and washed by foam. Stumbled over cobbles on the island of Nantucket. Lost themselves in mists clinging at daybreak to mysteriously shaped objects. Hid among flowering shrubs guarding mansion gateways. Endured without complaint noontides baked by the sun, the dreaded three o'clock in the afternoon, early evenings heralding relief and nights of short respite alive with the call of cicadas. Sought the highest point where the State of Rhode Island stretched out before them. Swept through the mushroom woods of Vermont and lakes of New Hampshire — too small for so many fish. Peered into harbours at decks carpeted in shells. Passed over inns specializing in sea delicacies. Yet did not forsake the land which had given rise to the fatal clam fritters.

At last Phoebe fell asleep. She collapsed on the bedspread without undoing her corset or pinching shoes. Lay in a pool of hair long released from bondage in the bun, but paying for its unexpected freedom with the stench of the basin's contents. Brown fluid had dried on her right hand — icy cold as it clenched a corner of the sheet. Phoebe was dreaming : wandering down an ever narrower tunnel paved with slimy shells. When she reached the far end, or what she took for the time being to be the extent of her roaming, she stood before a green, pulsating door. She had barely opened it when she realised she'd let herself be caught in a trap. Then she was falling for hours, brushing against the undulating walls of the Earth's aorta as it dragged her in deeper and deeper, as far as the loud beating heart. She knew if she was too late and didn't protect the heart from the army of sea monsters, the Earth would die along with her and the people imprisoned in its veins.

But she did not die. The following day she felt better already and her gruesome adventure would have sunk no doubt into oblivion, were it not for the talbotype made by an inquisitive photographer who happened to peer in the late afternoon through the windows of the houses on Benefit Street. Several factors came together serendipitously. First, Phoebe Hicks was poisoned by a piece of clam not long after the process patented in 1841 reduced the exposure time to three minutes. Her utter stillness over the washstand sufficed to capture the historic moment.

Second, William Henry Fox Talbot's invention, in contrast to the daguerreotype, enabled the multiple printing of photographic images. Phoebe's fame was thus able to spread with a speed unimaginable a few years before.

Third, photographs developed according to this technique were characterized by fuzziness and gradual fading of the image caused by chemical decomposition. This fact also contributed to the consolidation of Phoebe's legend. Simple minds were convinced that spirits were bearing away with them into the Beyond a portrait of their earthly friend. The indistinct photograph in which, in the semi-transparent contents of the washbasin, someone happened to spot ectoplasm emerging from the mouth of the future medium opened for Phoebe the gateway to an unexpected career.

ECTOPLASM

The unanswered questions mounting around Phoebe Hicks have their origin in the interpretation of the prying photographer's picture. Studies of Spiritualism cite 1894 as the date when the phenomenon of spiritual energy manifesting itself as ectoplasm (or "exteriorized matter" from the Greek words *ektos* and *plasma*) was first described. With excessive precision, historians of Spiritualism record accounts of eruptions of a white, warm, mucous-like substance unpleasant to the touch, which shines in the dark, transforms under the influence of light, occasionally assumes the form of a human face and smells of ozone, oozing from the mouth, nose, ears, belly-button, nipples and sometimes the vagina of the medium steeped in trance. Among the conditions conducive to the birth of ectoplasm, they mockingly list darkness, religious songs that drown out other sounds, and the physical distance separating the medium from the rest of the assembly. They describe sadomasochistic photographs, in which the medium — sitting transfixed in a dark room, her mouth tied with a gag — emits ectoplasm from between her parted legs. Occasionally she reclines, her face covered in a semi-transparent veil, while the "exteriorized matter" gushes from her wide-open mouth.

Researchers speculate about the speed with which the body of the guide to the Beyond reabsorbed the ectoplasm at the end of the séance. They dwell on the contrast between the aura of nineteenth-century parlours — where every knick-knack had its appointed place among the flounces, lace, cushions, mirrors, stuffed birds, footstools, and spiritualists buttoned to the neck and paralysed in their roles — and the young woman subjected to such intimate transmutations. They draw attention to the obvious reason why ectoplasm fulfilled the expectations of those seeking proof of the existence of the Other Side : thanks to it, what had hitherto been elusive — had now become tangible.

Why, however, do scholars pass over in silence the earliest known case, that of Phoebe? Why is it that when discussing methods practised by frauds to make ectoplasm (from muslin, cheesecloth, satin, soap, paper, egg white, potato flour, gelatine, giblets, calf or pig lungs), they suppress information about its first photographic record? Many historians working independently of one another repeat such oversights. Perhaps it's not too late though to recreate the history of Phoebe Hicks, restore her historical significance?

THE SCHEDULE OF SÉANCES

On 2 December 1847 Phoebe Hicks conducted her first séance — still tentative, in a room not entirely blacked out, with the participation of not the most aptly chosen guests, who proved to be more a hindrance than a help. A second séance followed, already more accomplished, and then a third, even more successful. And as to subsequent ones . . .

During the fourth, guided by an internal impulse, Phoebe introduced a rule observed afterwards by her successors that séances should always be held at the same hour and in the same room. She sensed instinctively that spirits were attached even more than the living to particular places (hence the ghosts of former inhabitants harassing the old houses), and that the stale aura prevailing beyond the grave made them value well-ventilated rooms. Levitating mediums would take advantage of this knowledge and even in late autumn leave open a parlour window. To the astonishment of the assembled participants, they could then fly out of it and back in at will.

Phoebe's séances — like those of mediums that came after her — took place at round or oval tables supported by a sculpted leg (replaced later by frauds with smaller tables on wheels). Starting from the fifth séance, Phoebe invited an uneven number of guests. The ideal group, she believed, consisted of four gentlemen and four ladies, including the medium. Phantoms apparently favoured clear divisions. If there were more participants, they never exceeded a total of twelve. The erotic charge emitted by touching palms, knees and feet conferred an additional earthly quality on the meetings of spiritualists of both sexes, who on the medium's request always sat alternately : woman, man, woman, man. The rule that no séance should last for more than two hours was a sign of respect to visitors from the Beyond. Spirits, according to Phoebe, were endowed with less patience than the living. Their behaviour could be just as unpredictable as that of the magic town's inhabitants. Now and again they appeared with some object in their hands that had originated in their former stay on earth, as though their families weren't otherwise capable of recognizing with whom they were dealing. Other times they'd make their presence felt only by a smell, light, or a kind of foreboding suddenly descending upon one of the guests.

Phoebe's fame spread swiftly across New England. Her séances were the talk of five-o'clock teas, whispered over during too long Sunday services or evening strolls amid colonial houses. Dockhands shouted to one another about them in the ports. Those who'd taken part for the first time would relate endlessly how the heads bent over the table seemed so lonely, as if suspended in the air around the gleam of light shed by the oil lamp, liberated from constraining hands, legs, bellies, throats and backs of necks. Free yet incomplete, hardly begun. Because the impression they'd been guillotined seemed to belong more to the world of the dead than the living. Reminiscent of Catholic saints in the moment before martyrdom : staring eyes, half-open lips, a glimmer behind in the shape of a halo. Some people compared the collected face of the medium, as if amputated and set against the dark background, to a blob of ectoplasm.

Phoebe marvelled at the attention the newspapers devoted to her. She had no time to reflect, however, upon the strange mechanisms of fame — so many new responsibilities rested upon her.

Though she preferred to entertain guests in her own home, some invitations she could not refuse. So if on Monday she was to take part in a séance at the house of Mr and Mrs B., her neighbours on Benefit Street, then she knew that on Tuesday she would have to accept the invitation of their relative Mr C., fortunately also residing nearby like everyone else in Providence, which in turn entailed the necessity of conjuring up, on Wednesday, the spirit of the prematurely deceased brother of Miss K., a spinster living out her days in solitude in the neglected family mansion. And though the elaborate iron fencing and widow's walk, grander than any other in the neighbourhood, still recalled their former glory, the house's location entirely harmonized with the melancholy of its owner. The windows overlooking St John's Cemetery conferred upon the séances an atmosphere Phoebe did not like. Her ease in establishing contact with spirits was not at all accompanied by the pleasure some folk derive from the tranquillity of cemetery alleyways.

THE MOSQUITO

Phoebe Hicks's first trance was interrupted by a mosquito. No one knew how it flew into the darkened room, drunk on human blood, since the windows were shut, heavy blinds drawn — and it was too late in the year for mosquitoes. Witnesses to this historic event claimed later that it was not of this world, that the spirit of a local pastor conjured up earlier had materialised in it. They maintained that Phoebe had not heard the pastor out, so he'd returned in the form of an insect to prevent other spirits from telling their stories. Although this theory seems to have been a hoax, many mediums afterwards feared the buzzing of insects would ruin their concentration.

WHO WAS PHOEBE HICKS?

When Phoebe Hicks conducted her first séance, when she became the first medium in New England, when her fame began to entice other women to embark on a similar career, no one foresaw, of course, what would distinguish her from her successors. This difference, not so crucial at first glance, fundamentally influenced Phoebe's story. Thanks to her good birth into a well-to-do home on Benefit Street, Phoebe Hicks enjoyed a financial independence rarely accessible to women in those days. As fate would have it, her parents died — poisoned by crab meat, according to rumour — leaving a fortune she did not have to share with non-existent siblings or cousins. At the age of thirty-three, the unmarried Phoebe knew her future was secure and life would drift on as in an uncapsizable boat lined with down. Few mediums could afford to reject marriage, which Spiritualism saw as the main source of restrictions on a woman's freedom. Phoebe Hicks along with Achsa White Sprague, who would be miraculously cured from a longstanding debilitating illness and famous for her public speeches uttered in trance, belong to that small group of female spiritualists deaf to the declarations of wealthy suitors.

Phoebe's conjuring of spirits, materialisations and levitations were the product of boredom, a sense of theatre, or of actual contacts with the Beyond. Séances brought her amusement, local renown, the interest of newspapers, admiration of many ladies and gentlemen, disapproval of conservative citizens, but no profit measurable in monetary terms or improvement in social status. Thus she sometimes allowed herself extravagances without caring what her guests would say. The phantoms she conjured caused bewilderment among the spiritualists sitting motionless in the dark rather than answered their questions.

The mediums who followed her, coming from modest families and treating Spiritualism as a path to social advancement, could not afford such luxury. They could not refuse — as Phoebe did — invitations to participate in public trances organized in town halls hundreds of miles apart. Such spectacles brought financial gain, satisfaction (these were the first public speeches delivered by women) but also the risk of suffering humiliation before an audience. And though in the eyes of many critics of the new fashion accepting a fee was evidence of fraud, the majority of mediums were unable to turn it down. Exhausting journeys and the abuse of alcohol, intended to enhance their visions, were the daily bread of thousands of women whose vocation of "medium" found its way into the official list of American professions only a few years after Phoebe Hicks consumed the spoiled clam.

Phoebe meanwhile wished to hear neither of public performances nor excursions away from the magic town of Providence. She selected carefully the participants for her gatherings. Accounts of the goings-on in her house exceeded in folly and imagination descriptions of other séances, conducted with the expectations of wealthy benefactors in mind.

And though malicious folk whispered that the success of her séances depended on the paucity of other attractions in the town of Providence, it's not worth paying heed to wicked tongues.

FEVER

As the fashion for Spiritualism spread across New England, mediums introduced the custom of beginning séances with a prayer and the singing of a hymn. Phoebe was the only one who refrained, thereby exposing herself to the criticism of God-fearing citizens. Younger mediums patiently served apprenticeships with persons more experienced in spirit communication. With Phoebe alone such knowledge was innate. She later recalled that when she discovered it within herself shortly after being poisoned, she felt as if suddenly struck by high fever. From then on, the sensation always accompanied her in the climactic moments of séances.

In mesmerism the female medium was an obedient tool in the hands of an often erotically inclined hypnotist. Spiritualism gave the medium power. Phoebe quickly grasped this. She understood that summoning spirits was a way for wives and old maids condemned to domestic boredom to momentarily step outside their usual roles. An escape into the Unknown, to which a woman, stifled in the daytime, became a guide. The subsequent shift in the balance of power at the table from the perorating gentlemen, so self-assured a moment earlier, to the silent lady concentrating upon herself the submissive, expectant gazes once the lamps were lowered, was impressive. That many mediums did not wear corsets during séances came not only from the banal desire to win over male spiritualists with a little more than just promises of contacts with the Beyond. The rejection of the corset was also an act of liberation and return to the physical body forbidden by Victorian morality. Still braver mediums appealed to spirits to help them shed any garments whatsoever. Dematerialisations of earthly wardrobes were not uncommon.

Sometimes, liberation went considerably further when, on the instigation of a spiritual guide, a medium left her husband and even joined her life — not quite openly — to that of another woman. Female spiritualists stuck in unhappy relationships were occasionally advised to follow a similar path.

The only known case of violent conflict between mediums apparently had its source in the antagonism between the spiritual guides manipulating them. The clash between two New York mediums was discussed at length by the spiritualist magazines. Miss F. escaped with a lacerated ear. Her adversary's broken arm required medical attention.

Yet the anecdotal history of the movement should not overshadow its political significance. The Victorian imagination was fascinated by the apparitions of American Indians and black slaves passing through many séances. Cora Maynard, Abraham Lincoln's favourite medium — visiting the White House after the death of one of his sons — believed the spirits she summoned hastened the issuing of the Emancipation Proclamation.

A courage and nobility unknown to whites characterized the red-skinned phantoms. The séances they participated in offered longed-for therapy to descendants of Old World immigrants worn down by feelings of guilt.

It's no accident that the birth of Spiritualism coincided with the publication of the *Declaration of Sentiments*, modelled on the *Declaration of Independence* and recognizing women's citizenship rights for the first time. Not all suffragettes were spiritualists, but the majority of both female and male spiritualists fought for women's autonomy in marriage and the right to divorce. Packed to the brim, American assembly halls in the 1850s and 60s became tribunes of progressive ideas expressed by mediums immersed in trance. Spiritualism challenged social norms to the same degree as the women's emancipation movement.

Aware of all these nuances, Phoebe made three historic pronouncements. The first : "A few vibrations do not a medium make," was a criticism of her successors trying to master too swiftly the arcana of a difficult art, while the second : "A medium's talent is like an unbroken steed," alluded to the fact that mediums, before they come to the aid of others, ought to work on themselves. Devoid of control, their gift was often dangerous.

Her vision that "Spiritualism will be universal or will not be at all," proved correct : for decades to come Spiritualism was to occupy the minds of American puritans more than any other movement. As it fell out of vogue, mediums had to seek new occupations. From their former profession they supposedly retained a liking for hashish, opium, marijuana and other unnamed narcotics.

The unexpected beneficiaries of contacts with the other side turned out to be cooks, for more than a hundred years exploring recipes supplied by phantoms, their flavours oscillating between the preferences of the dead and those of the living.

Like the spirits, some mediums were corpulent, good-natured matrons whose physicality presented an amusing contrast to their esoteric calling. Kind-heartedness occasionally prompted them to confess to confidants the secrets of their profession : for the sake of their clients, they enacted a comedy. Just as certain women feign orgasm so as not to wound the *amour propre* of their husbands or lovers, so mediums simulated trance to satisfy the expectations of séance participants. Comparisons between the séance and the act of love often featured in occultist discussions. The darkened room, physical contact of palms sweating from emotion, accelerated breathing, being wrenched from time and space, the heightened awareness of the other person, sensitivity to smell and the twitching of fingers, feelings of intimacy and shame, impatience and tension, tears of bliss — and the lump in the throat, the frustration, the sense of repugnance towards oneself and one's companions when the séance was not successful. And if it was — happiness and fulfilment, tinged with regret that it was now all over.

Phoebe knew that during a séance — just as during intercourse — the most important thing was concentration. Which is why so many women never achieve orgasm and so many mediums are doomed to fraud. They are unable to pinpoint the tenuous thread leading to the Beyond. And if they do, it writhes around too much, meanders in convoluted ways, or disappears too quickly over the horizon for any lover or medium to patiently follow. For Phoebe, in contrast, it was enough to concentrate her thoughts on moulding two seemingly identical little

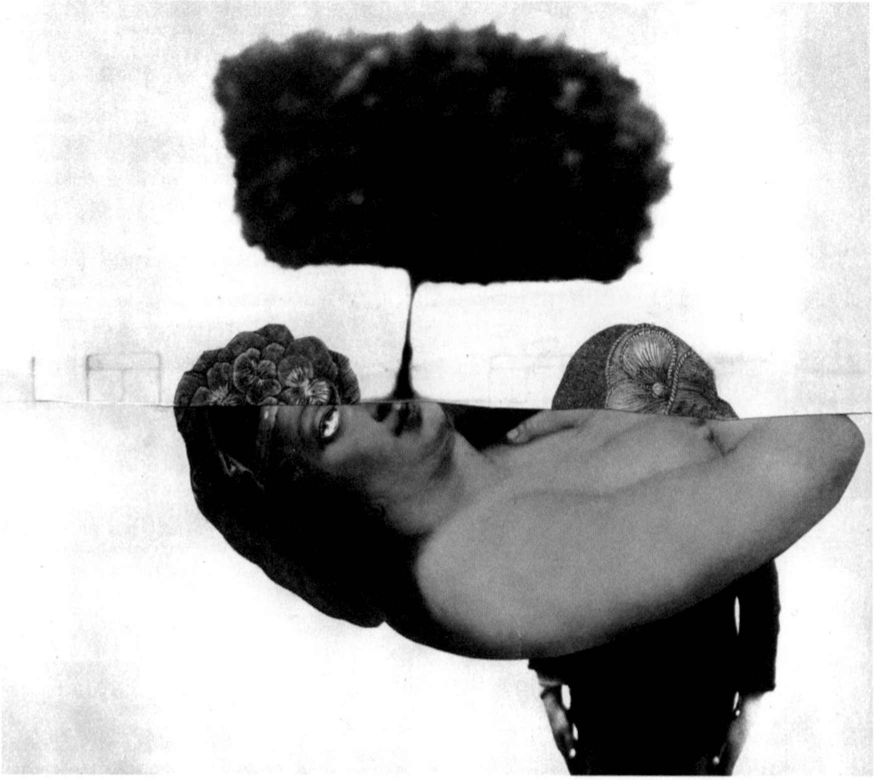

balls of bread. She had known this strange, physical sensation since childhood, but it was only later that she discovered its beneficial effect. From that moment on, whenever she sat at the table in the ring of joined hands, she thought of nothing except moulding the little balls. Sometimes she was tempted to whisper this simple method to other mediums exhausted by simulating trances, but did not do so out of embarrassment and because she knew that for them, balls of fresh bread might not possess the same power.

THE MAID

Participants in séances taking place at Phoebe's house were greeted in the doorway by Jonathan, the cook's son, a ten-year-old physically well-developed for his age. Awareness of how incongruous his stature was with his round baby face seemed to intimidate him and made his movements especially awkward. Without looking the guests in the eye, he would clumsily relieve them of their coats, hats and gloves and lead them into the dark interior, where the maid Miriam would take them under her wing. Her dignified presence made some mistake her for the mistress of the house. She never wore a white apron, while her black dress and greying hair tied back with a velvet ribbon imparted an elegance not normally encountered among servants. Yet such aristocratic bearing did not protect Miriam from the charge that she supplied her mistress, according to methods not openly discussed, with information later used in the séances. Sceptics even believed it was the maid's intelligence and not the exceptional talents of the medium that lay behind the latter's success. They accused her of practises employed by accomplices of other mediums to gain information about clients : bribing servants, placing "their people" in noisy inns where alcohol loosened tongues, studying gravestones — the most reliable sources of information about family relationships. They forgot that it sufficed to reside in Providence a little while to know enough about one's neighbours to imagine the rest. For the inhabitants of the magic town were strangely alike.

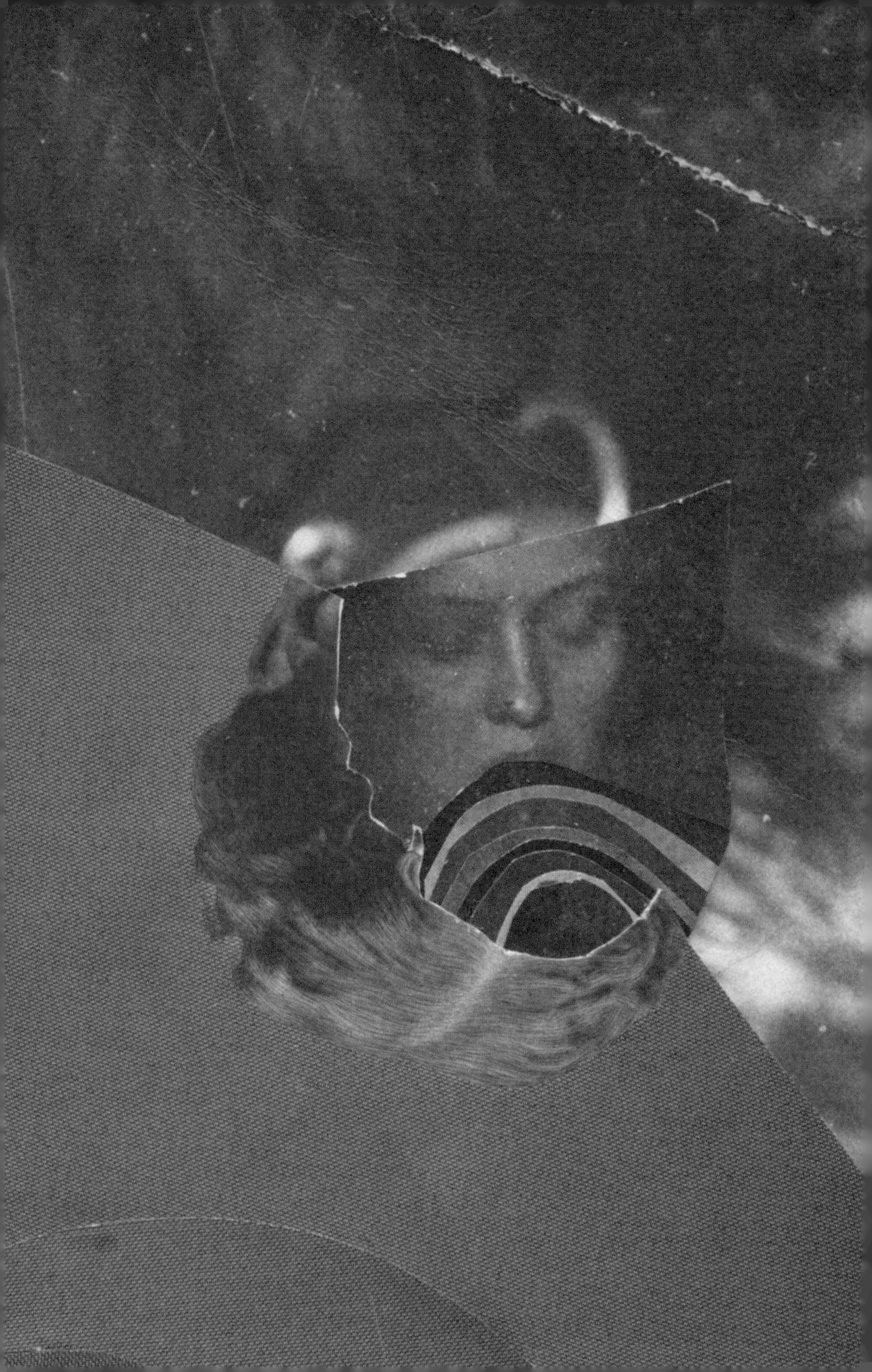

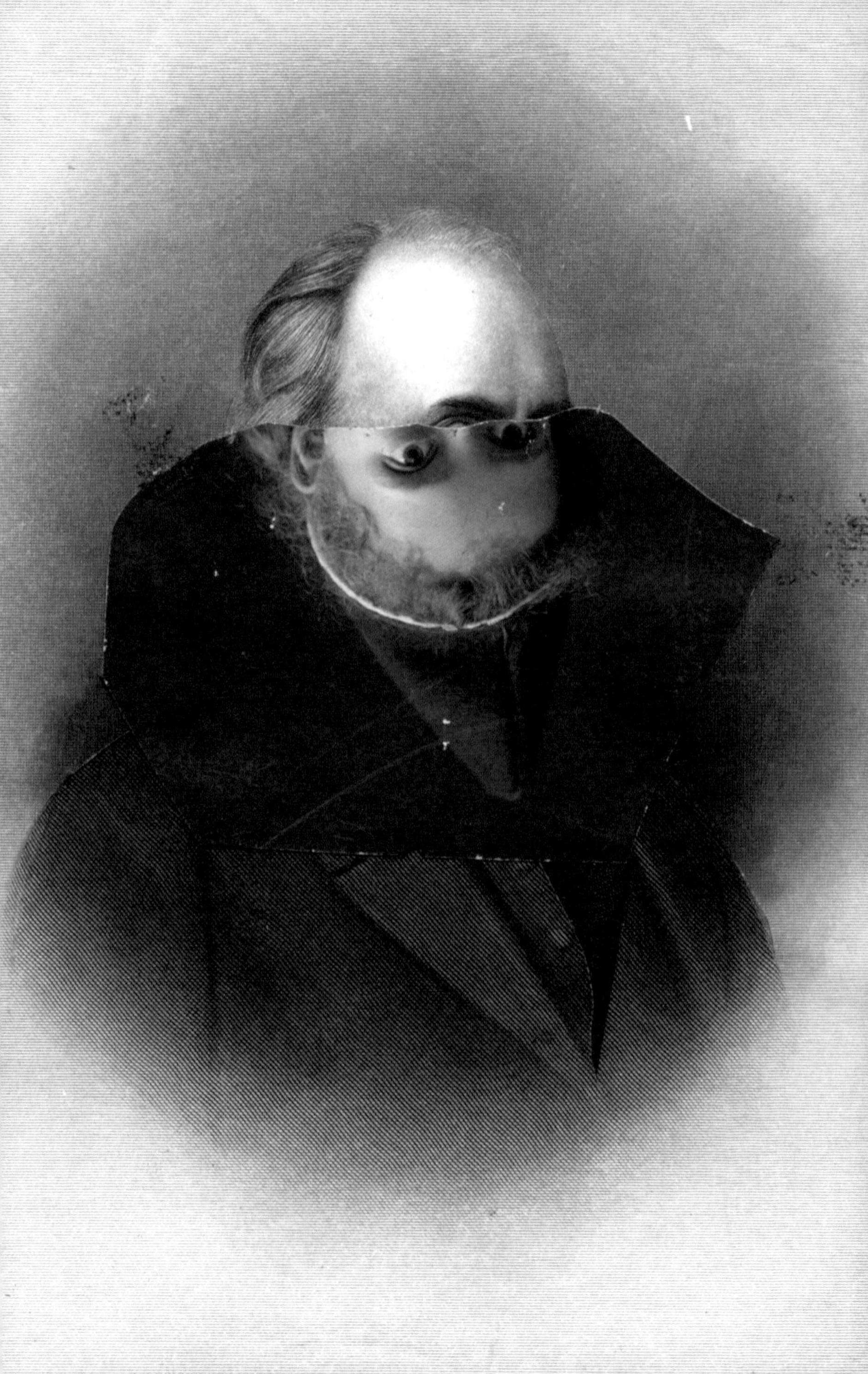

THE SCEPTICS

Phoebe Hicks instinctively recognized sceptics who doubted her powers. When such a person drew near, she felt nonexistent animal hair bristle all over her body — as though she were about to change into a dog, or cat, or rat, if only to avoid the mocking, inquisitive stare and uncomfortable questions. Such encounters rarely led to anything fine or interesting. Phoebe and her inquisitor had little to say to each other. Usually they parted hurriedly, faster than required by a good upbringing. If they remained together longer, a sense of tedium would descend, robbing Phoebe of any desire to convince the sceptic of her gift, and him of his eagerness to expose her fraud.

SOUNDS

Worse than sceptics were people endowed with high-pitched voices. Sounds — as is well known — permeate walls, while spirits have sensitive ears (significantly more sensitive than their eyes, on account of which they don't usually establish eye contact with the living). On Thursday evenings, long after the lights had been put out and virtual silence descended, the echo of Philip Craft's harangue interrupted by Suzanne Gable's nervous giggle would resound in the parlour. It's hardly surprising the spirits had no desire to visit that night and made Phoebe's guests wait longer than usual.

CRAMP

The most loyal séance participants could tell when a spirit was about to appear. Phoebe's left calf cramped on every visitation, and although she learned how to mask the pain, she could not fool her disciples. Immediately afterwards a chill breath would pass through the parlour announcing the climax was near. And so the materialisations were no great surprise to them. If there was anything astonishing, it was the forms assumed by figures from the Beyond.

THE HYPNOTIC STARE OF THE BEDOUIN

The second phase of Phoebe's fame — since the first, following her poisoning by the clam fritter, was not marked by anything special — was the Egyptian period. During this time, the medium and her guests experienced events hard to put down to fascination with a far-away country they knew almost nothing about — except, perhaps, that its sandy wastes resembled the dunes at Cape Cod.

It began with a caravan making its way across a desert. This procession — hardly to be expected in the State of Rhode Island — interrupted the séance and took the mistress of the house as much by surprise as her guests. A moment later, a crescent moon blazed from the parlour ceiling. Grains of sand poured into the spiritualists' eyes. The whistle of the desert wind and the muezzin's cry drowned the crackling logs in the hearth. A camel walking past the pastor spat an inch above his head. A potted palm transformed into a minaret, and the minaret into a pyramid. The leafless trees outside the window were replaced by the blue sheet of the Nile. The colours of the saddlecloths on the camels' humps stunned the inhabitants of the magic town of Providence, unaccustomed to such intense dyes. As they squinted in the glare, the mirage of a crocodile's mummy flashed before their eyes. The stench of ammonia pervading the pyramid corridors rushed up their nostrils.

None of those present could later describe how long the Bedouin had tramped across the room. When the last camel had disappeared over the dunes, Phoebe bid her guests goodnight and turned them out into the April night. If, on the following

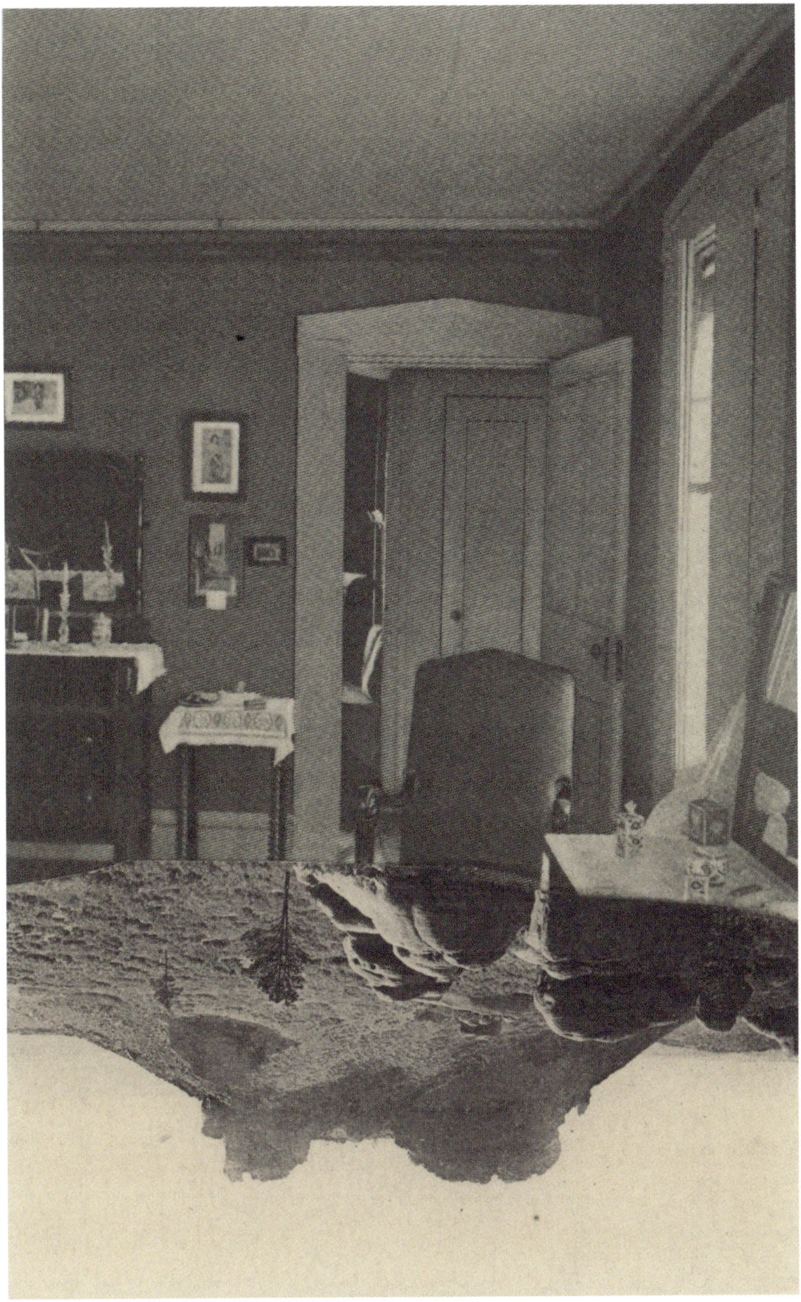

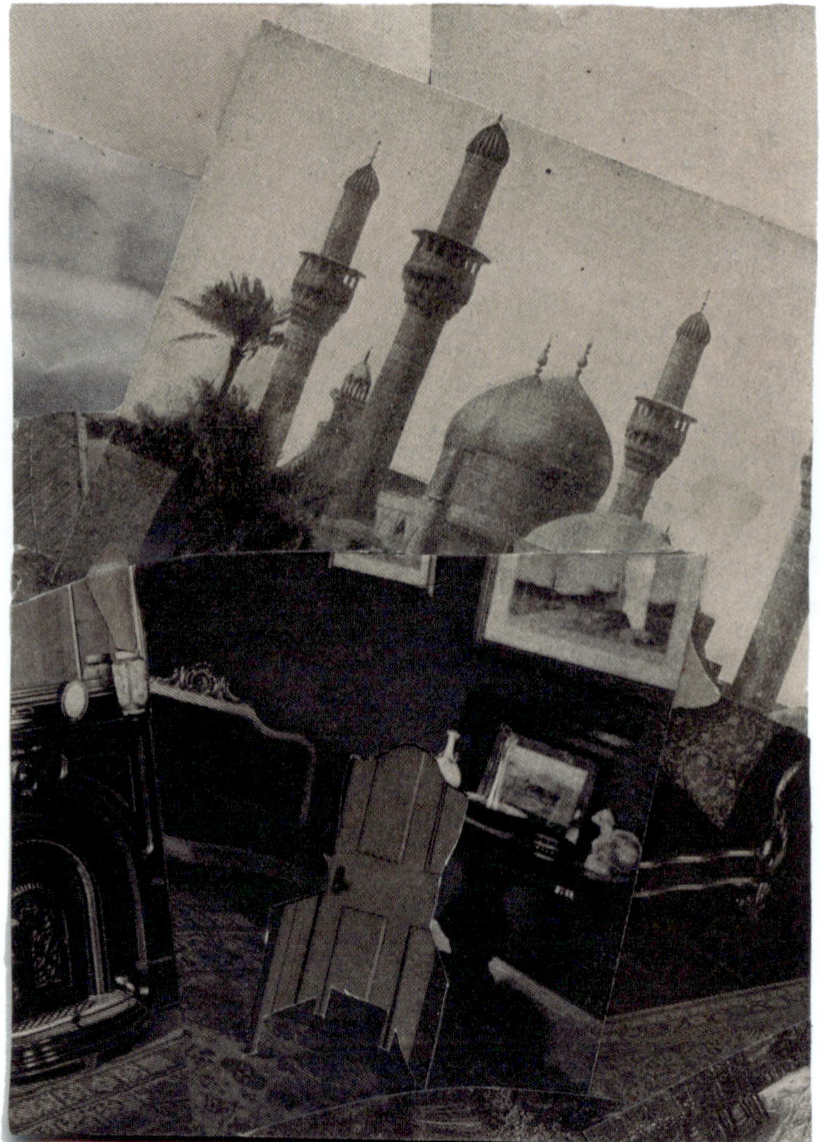

day, Howard Williams had not found a handful of sand in his frock-coat pocket, everyone would have regarded the event as a collective hallucination. Yet the passing caravan was only the prelude to an Egyptian invasion. On subsequent evenings Phoebe's parlour was visited by mummies levitating a few inches above the floor. One of the sceptics tried to grab the lowest one, but all that remained in his hand was a scrap of mouldy bandage which instantly crumbled to dust.

A few weeks later the spiritualists — less and less surprised now by exotic visits — were brought the spirit of Hatshepsut, a female Pharaoh who died in mysterious circumstances, as well as the sphinx who guarded her tomb. Hatshepsut remained silent, but the sphinx proved so talkative it exhausted the New England puritans more than the flitting mummies. No doubt, it was this weariness that drove the Egyptian ghosts away to the séances of other mediums. A lasting consequence of that period was the madness of Mrs Howard Williams. For the remaining twenty-seven years of her life, the hypnotic stare of the Bedouin followed her day and night. Explanations that the caravan's march past had taken place on April 1, and so should not be taken too seriously, fell on deaf ears.

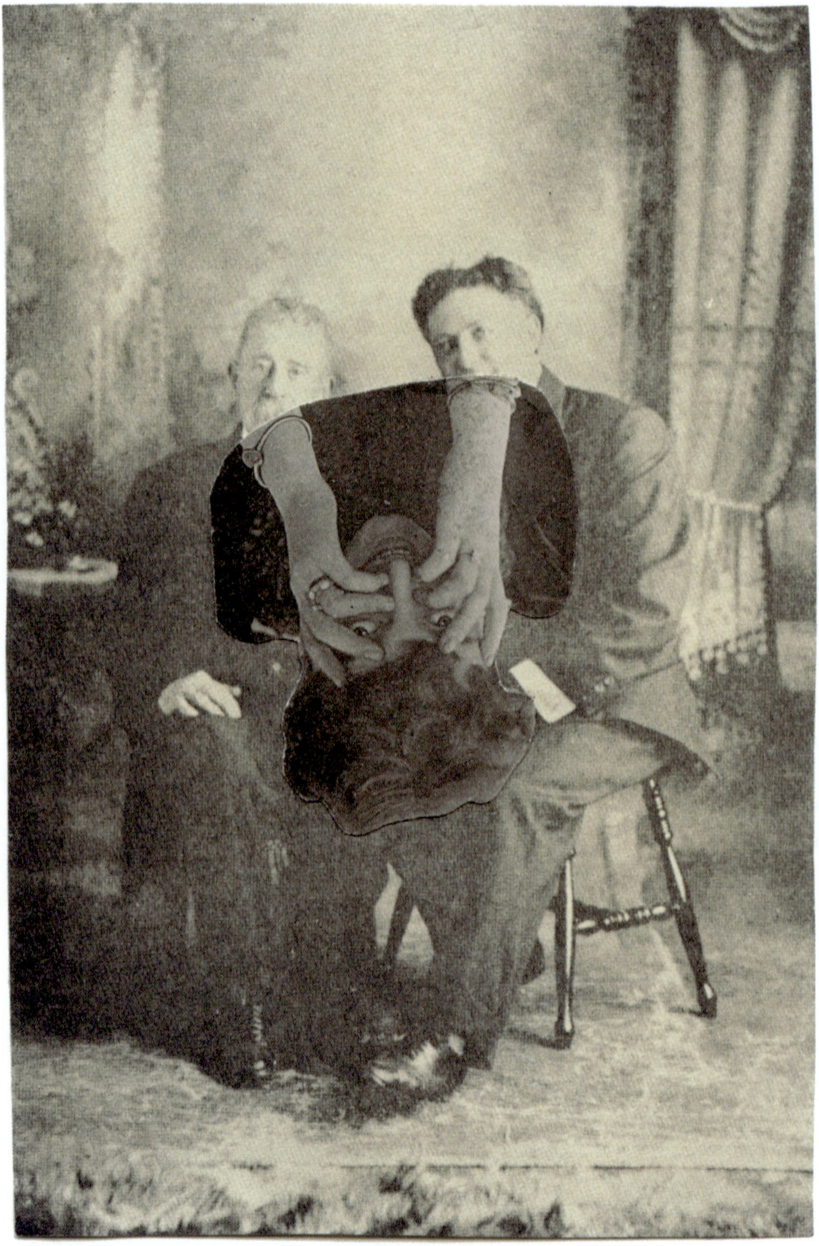

MATERIALISATION FROM THE AZURE PLASMA

The spirit of Harry Houdini inaugurated the third phase of Phoebe's fame. He joined the séance by materializing out of an azure cloud hovering over the table, which some took for ectoplasm. He remained with the company throughout sixteen long evenings, sometimes looming out of the plasma, sometimes stepping from behind a heavy curtain concealed in the gloom, sometimes emerging from under the plush drape spread over the table. Before the start of the final séance with his participation, he sat at Phoebe's right, awaiting the guests like any legitimate citizen of this world. It could be argued of course he was merely the medium's assistant dressed as a magician, sitting shoulder to shoulder with the others, emboldened by their gullibility. Yet how to interpret his materialisations from the azure cloud? Explain the appearance of the ghost of someone born a quarter-century later? And what possible interest could the medium have had in fighting a duel of magic tricks with Houdini, which would only compromise her in the eyes of spiritualists?

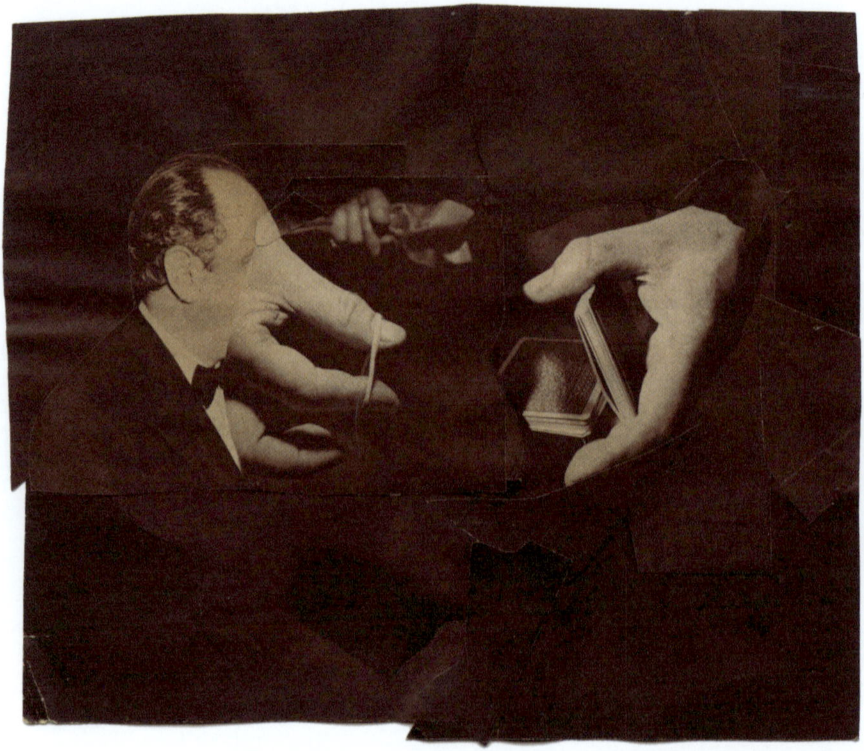

PHOEBE VS. HOUDINI

Nothing augured Phoebe's duel with Harry Houdini. The magician's spirit started it suddenly during his sixteenth séance and then, two hours later, abandoned the bemused participants. Garbled tales of the duel circulated across New England for many years to come. It's not true the spirit jangled his chains. Nor was the medium irritated by the situation while he maintained a cold indifference. The only account anywhere close to the truth related how the two taunted one another : every time Phoebe caused a thing or person to materialise, Houdini made it disappear. The list of objects she conjured from the abyss is not long : a rusty teapot, a bouquet of dried yellow flowers and an antique Turkish carpet, which on closer examination would probably have proved a lousy fake. Figures momentarily summoned from the Other World included Ivan the Terrible, Catherine the Great and Alexander Pushkin, thereby confirming rumours about the weakness of American mediums for Russian culture. Be that as it may, Houdini did not allow any phantom who would testify to Phoebe's genius to remain among the living for more than a minute. Even in his ghostly form, the greatest unmasker of fraudulent mediums did not miss an opportunity to belittle Phoebe's merits.

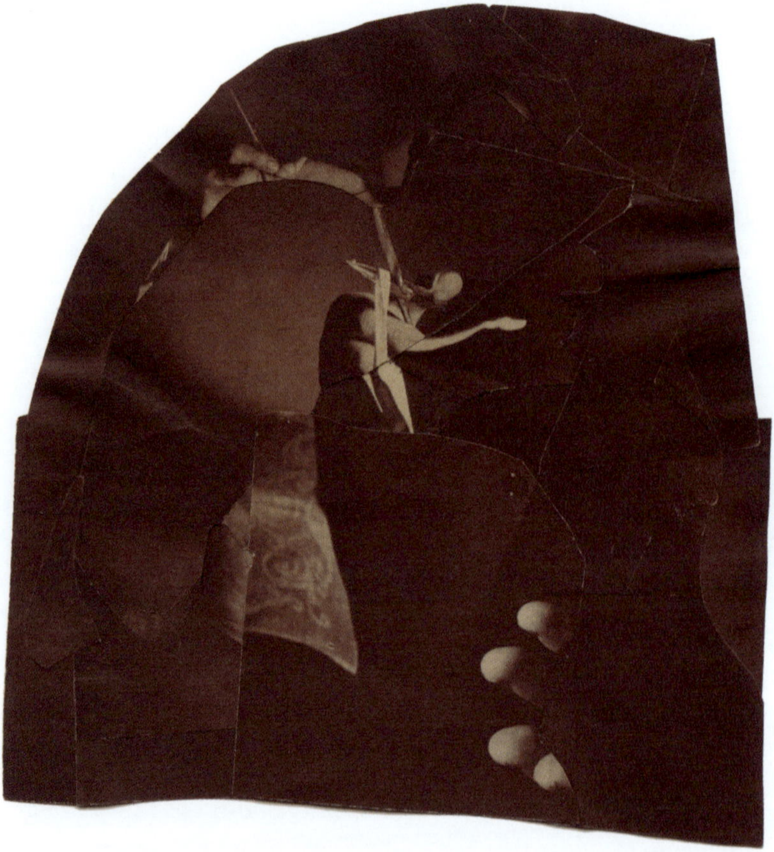

THE OIL LAMP

The duel between the famous medium and the spirit of the greatest illusionist of all time ended just as abruptly as it began. None of the assembly witnessed the phantom's final disappearance since it happened in total darkness. Phoebe maintained afterwards that when the Bedouin marched past earlier it caused Egyptian night to descend on the parlour. Whatever the reason, for the first and last time in Phoebe's career as a medium something happened that was very rare in nineteenth-century households accustomed to oil lamps : suddenly the lamp globe burst. No one had adjusted the flame. No one had even approached the elegant glass globe, etched in a rosebud design tastefully harmonizing with the colour of the drape. The blast was accompanied by a bang out of all proportion to the scale of the damage. The guests had scarcely torn their eyes from the phantom sitting in acrobatic pose to look at the lamp, when a draught emanating from nobody knew where made itself felt in the room, transforming in a split second into an icy breath. It extinguished the flame, putting an end to the tension. In the last flash of light, the master of underwater escapes was seen doubled up in pain — then he vanished through the window. For a moment, his silhouette remained visible in the fog. Soon utter darkness fell. Only eighty years later did readers of accounts of Phoebe's séances understand the meaning of the spirit's gesture : it was a premonition of Houdini's tragic end from a punch to the stomach. For a long time his admirers could not believe in such an unexpected death. Phoebe had no difficulty in predicting it.

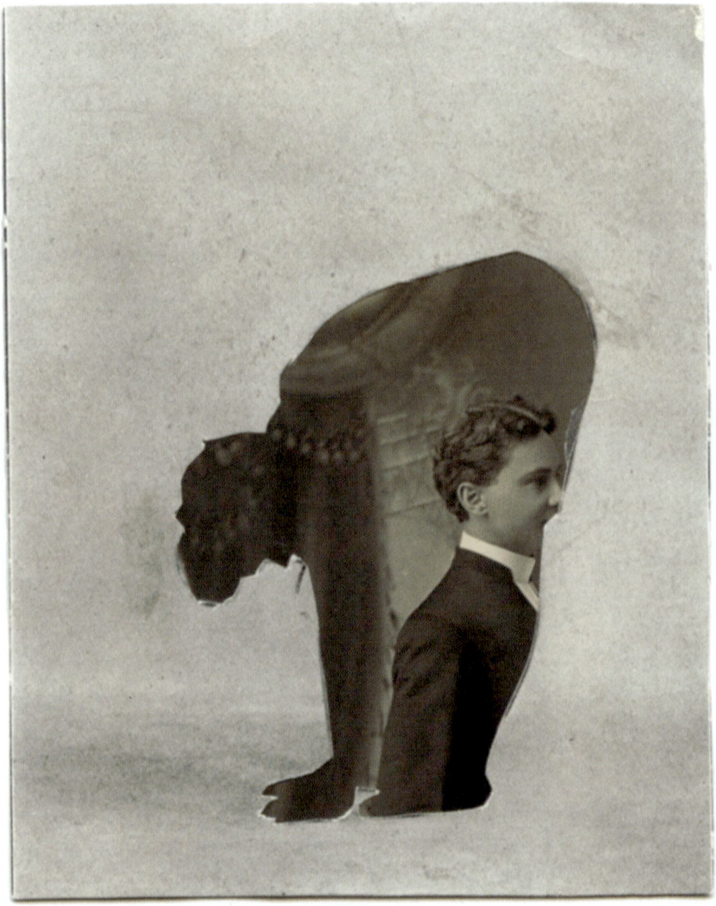

THE NOSE

The most curious event in the spiritualist practise of Phoebe Hicks was the manifestation of the Nose. It materialised towards the close of the sixty-sixth séance when the guests, wearied by a lack of response from the Beyond, were about to disband and go home. Moments before the clock struck ten-thirty semi-transparent plasma began to emerge from Phoebe's mouth, arousing consternation among first-time participants. The birth of the plasma lasted a good half hour, since wreathes of cotton-wool-like material were still emanating from the medium's mouth when eleven chimed. When it looked as though the table and ring of hands were about to disappear beneath it, the plasma broke away from Phoebe and slid off the tabletop with a nasty squelch. Once on the floor, it seemed to go on growing, though this was an illusion since it was merely seeking a place to fully materialise.

The parlour was spacious enough for the peregrinations of the obviously disturbed plasma to last until eleven-thirty. Absorbed by the spectacle, the spiritualists paid no attention to the passing of time. Only Phoebe's cat arched its back, snorted and retreated under a chair. Having chosen at last the oval carpet by the fireplace, the plasma stopped, coughed and began to assume the contours of a Nose — a huge upturned honker with a brown wart at its tip. Suspense rose among the witnesses and Phoebe's astonishment intensified as she struggled to observe the metamorphosis, exhausted by sitting for so long with her mouth open. The transformation was accompanied by sucking sounds — like when you stick your finger in a jar of jam. When the Nose was almost fully formed, the remaining traces of plasma tried to hide under the carpet but it called them to heel by clearing its throat. Midnight struck. The Nose rebuked the stupefied guests with a glare. By now it had reached the height of the tallest participant in the sixty-sixth séance.

Interpreters of Phoebe's mediumistic history later claimed the visitation of the Nose proved her ability to govern not only the world of apparitions, but also of literature. For indeed : barely had the Nose assumed its full proportions, when a briefcase appeared under the arm sprung from its left lobe, as did a pair of horn-rimmed eyeglasses above the wart and decorations covering most of the pale surface of its skin. Fortunately, the séance participants did not arouse its interest and the unpleasant visit quickly drew to a close. It managed to jot down a few denunciations in the notebook it had taken from the briefcase, swept another devastating glance over the company, with a gesture brooking no resistance pushed aside the maid, who, though having seen a thing or two in this household, was standing in the middle of the salon frozen in amazement, strode vigorously through to the hall, opened the front door and disappeared into the night. No one had enough presence of mind to spring to their feet, rush to the window and watch it move off past the quaint colonial houses of Benefit Street.

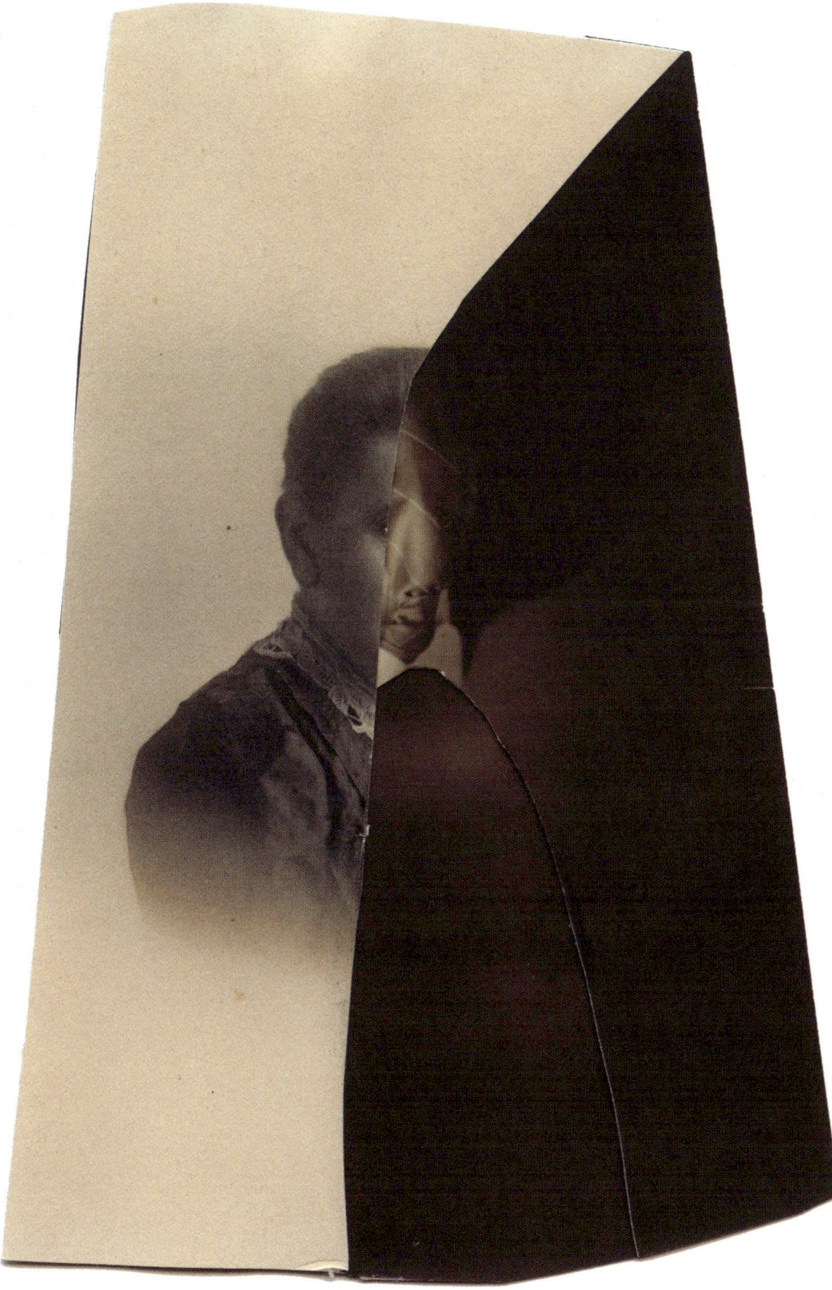

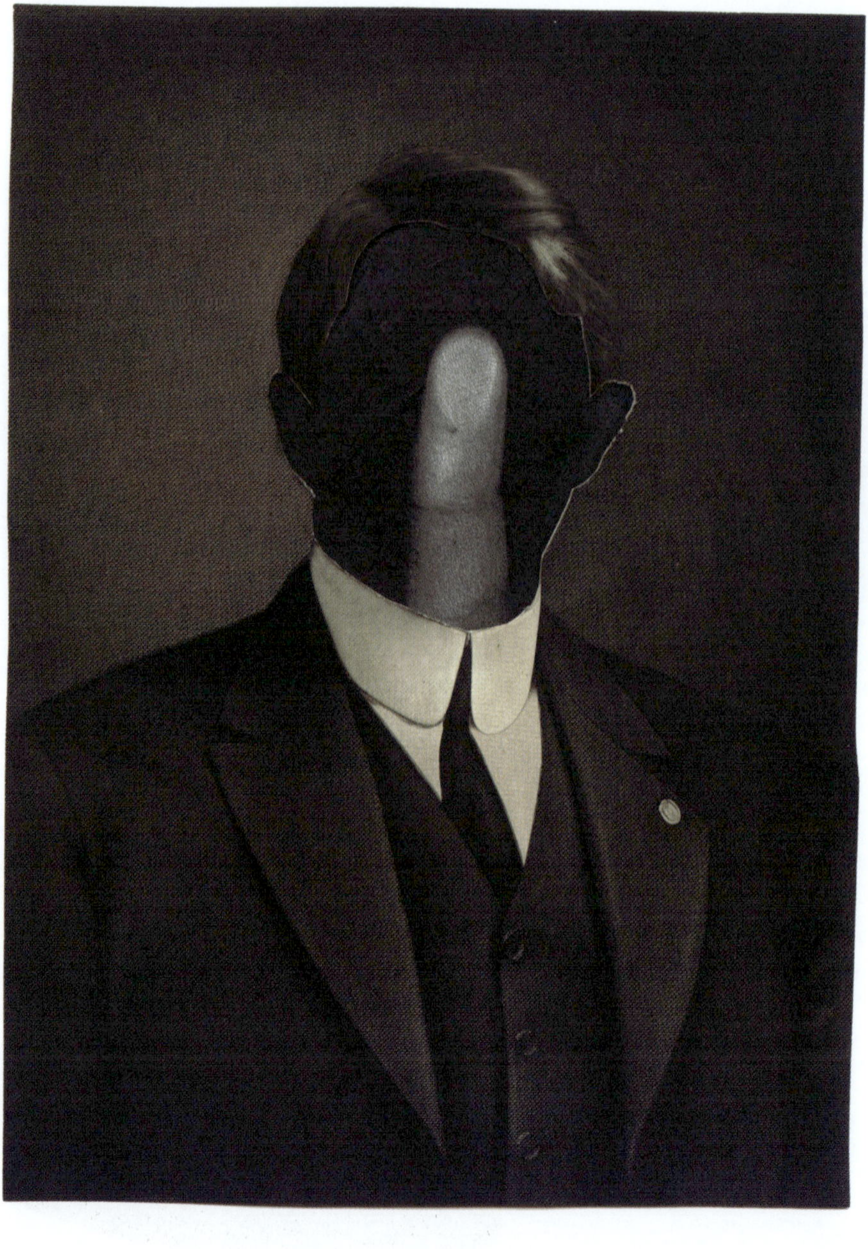

THE TOOTH

Witnesses to the sixty-sixth séance had not yet shaken off the impression left by the visitation of the Nose when the sixty-seventh meeting brought no less a surprise. The same people were present, plus a married couple travelling through Providence, drawn by curiosity about the medium's fame. This time plasma began to billow from Phoebe's ears even before everyone was seated comfortably at the table. The eruption was shorter than the previous evening, but the effect proved equally spectacular. Before seven witnesses (the absolute consistency of the accounts proves their authenticity) a Tooth of extraordinary proportions hatched out of the gelatinous mass. As if the phantoms were not content to make fun of the spiritualists by introducing the Nose! The Tooth, like the Nose, threw the company into confusion. And since Phoebe's guests were hardly in their first flush of youth and had all lost at least one tooth, the thought dawned on everyone : is this the ghost of my Tooth? Has it come to remind me of its right of return to the empty gap, shrunken in the meantime under pressure from its shamelessly expanding neighbours? Has it taken the trouble to migrate from the Beyond in order to wreak vengeance on its former keeper who had not cared sufficiently for its welfare? Or extort a promise to take better care of its remaining brothers and sisters? Such thoughts made this séance one of the least successful. Some participants even declined to repeat the experiment. And since Phoebe was both a practical woman and a good psychologist, as soon as she saw the Tooth taking shape in front of the sideboard, she knew some of her guests, instead of attending the next séance, would head for the dentist.

THE SPIRIT OF LEONORA DE LA CRUZ

Of the figures drawn by Phoebe from the Beyond, several were literary. The Spanish visionary nun, who slept through a large portion of her life dreaming prophetic dreams and was known in the nineteenth century only to a few bookworms, manifested herself in all her glory during a certain September séance. She began by driving out once and for all the spirit of the fair but gruesome Elizabeth, Countess Báthory, atoning beyond the grave for the murder of hundreds of young women in whose blood she had bathed to preserve her beauty. Initially, Phoebe's consternation was aroused by the rare event of a squabble between phantoms. On closer inspection of the victorious phantasm, the medium's astonishment mounted when she saw its likeness to herself! Phoebe knew many spiritualists would find in this coincidence endorsement of the rumours about her dishonest practises. All the more rapidly therefore, she let go the hand of the pastor sitting next to her and turned up the lamp flame. In its light the assembled guests observed the sisterly likeness more distinctly. They also satisfied themselves their hostess still occupied the place of honour at the table. Even the most ardent sceptics ruled out her incarnation in a ghost. Hardly had the phantom materialised sufficiently for the Carmelite habit and pilgrim's shell from Santiago de Compostela held in its hand to become visible, when, without waiting for questions, it began to enumerate in a monotonous voice the various catastrophes awaiting the twentieth century. The sinking of the Titanic, the Hindenburg disaster and several other tragedies, about which neither the medium nor her guests wished to hear.

And so for the first and last time in her mediumistic career Phoebe interrupted the visionary mid-stream and sent her back to the Other World. The sitters heaved a sigh of relief. Only at their next meeting did the well-read Emily Brown recall the heroine of a justly forgotten eighteenth-century French novel of unknown provenance, Leonora de la Cruz. The medium's amazement that a fictional figure could look like a twin sister knew no bounds!

How surprised were Phoebe's guests when they showed up one February day at the regular hour and discovered nothing in her house looked as it had until then. The furniture was positioned differently, the pictures were hanging somewhere else, even the carpets weren't lying where they had been for the last thirty years. Not so much the scale of the changes struck the spiritualists as their irrationality. The sideboard now stood in the middle of the parlour, the bed blocked the bedroom doorway, lamps thrust into corners lit up spiders' webs, carpets — rolled up against walls — only half-covered the floors. Exhausted but happy, Phoebe confessed it was spirits that had made her rearrange the rooms. And although one guest did not spare his malicious taunts, he quickly forgot his scepticism when the evening's séance proved to be an extraordinary experience. As if the spirits were gratefully repaying the medium for her obedience. It was precisely at this point that the ghost of the last Inca princess, Umina, stabbed a half century before in a Carpathian castle far removed from Peru or Providence, swept through the parlour. The phantom admittedly said nothing but its costume and trickle of blood oozing from the heart region left no doubt as to who had visited the medium's rearranged house. After that night Phoebe concluded the furniture, carpets and lamps could return to their former places. It was a wrong decision, since following the Incan princess's visit the spirits of boring and garrulous characters began to haunt the séances. These visitations became so tiresome several guests moved to other mediums. A simple discovery put an end to those trying weeks of Phoebe's career : it was enough to place some piece of furniture obliquely across the room, tilt a picture on the wall, make the carpet bulge, for phantoms to appear — in response to the spiritualists' summons — not only with unconventional looks and fascinating histories but also intriguing reflections on the theme of Eternity. Hence Phoebe deduced that people after death have a greater taste for disorder than order. Her desire to afford the spirits pleasure justified the chaos reigning in her house from then on.

One evening, two guests arriving early spied on Phoebe as she adopted poses in pictures hanging on the walls. When questioned as to why, she gave an evasive yet predictable explanation: spirits had instructed her to impersonate now Saint George, now the maiden he rescued, now the dragon belching fire. The incident was brought up later as rumours spread around Providence about Phoebe's ambitions, allegedly impelling her to enact séance comedies. Such gossip did nothing to diminish the faith of her most loyal frequenters.

LEVITATIONS

On one issue accounts of the séances are inconsistent : Did Phoebe Hicks, on some evenings, really levitate, after which — irrespective of the weather — she flew out of the window? Maybe the ladies and gentlemen who insisted it was true had let themselves be influenced by tales of Daniel Dunglas Home, who flew up into the air at any opportunity. Perhaps by speculating about levitation, séance veterans were trying to draw attention to themselves. Certainly prolonged sitting in the dark was conducive to hallucinations. Maybe as they rubbed their fingers, grown numb from remaining in the same position, Phoebe's guests longed for the séance to finally end. The medium's flying out of the room must have seemed to them not a bad solution. Or maybe the wind, usually blowing in this maritime town, caused the heavy curtain covering the window to stir, producing an illusion of movement. It remains a mystery whether Phoebe really did rise from the table as if asleep and, ignoring her guests' agitation, gradually take off from the floor, hover above the patterned carpet and heads of the spiritualists, change position over the table from vertical to horizontal, either growing in height or shrinking to the size of a child, only to disappear without a word of explanation, first among the folds of the curtain and then beyond the window.

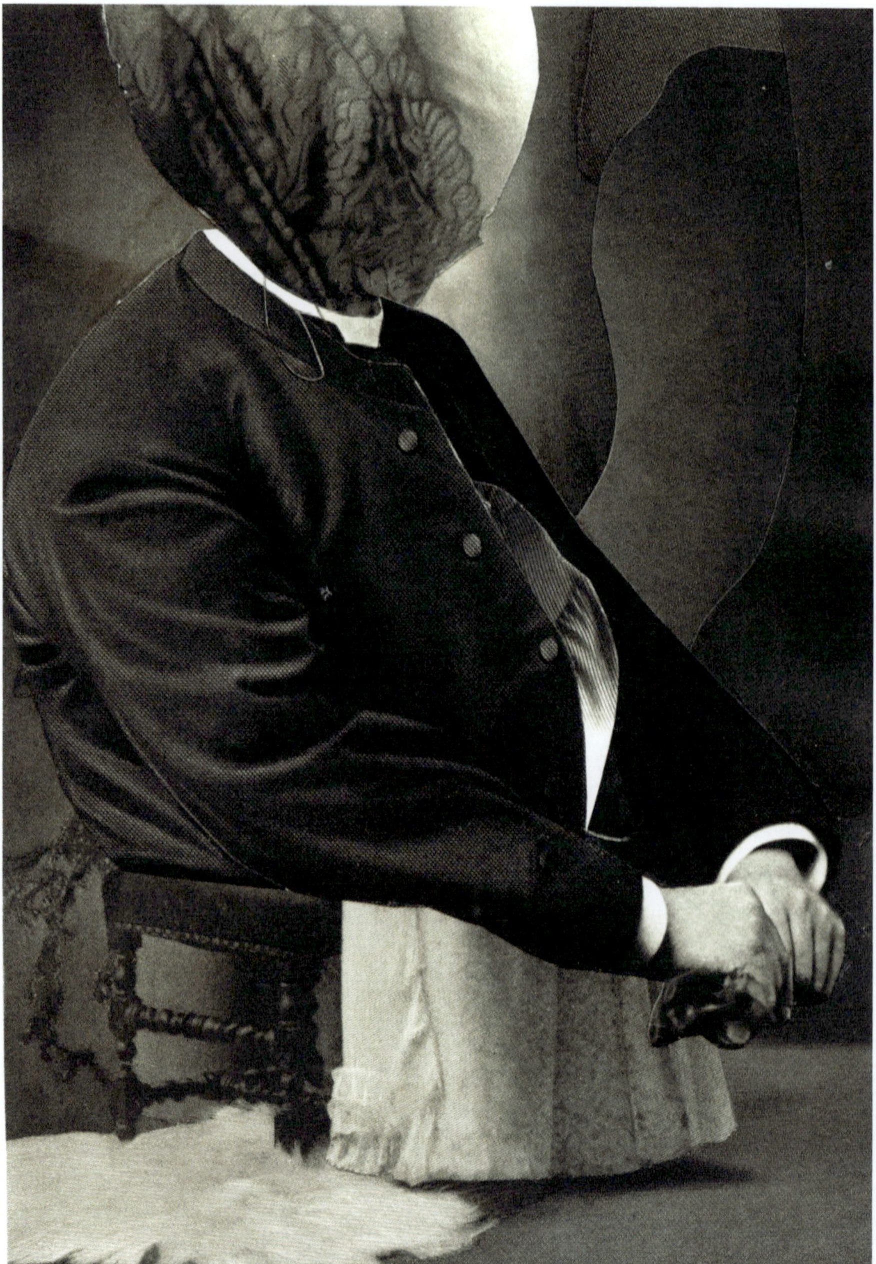

MATERIALISATIONS, TRANSFORMATIONS, APPORTS

The materialisation of an unnamed archbishop in liturgical robes left a deep impression on Phoebe's court. It was an occurrence all the more extraordinary since higher ranks of the Catholic clergy were seldom seen in her parlour. The phantom too must have felt out of place. After its brief sojourn among the living, it began to shrink violently, maintaining however the former proportions of the archbishop, who in life had been five foot five inches tall. Having shrunk to a height of four inches, it delivered a sermon too abstruse for the present company, after which it vanished completely. Its disappearance was accelerated by the intervention of a dentist participating in the séance who, unmoved by the medium's protests and succumbing to his professional curiosity, attempted to ascertain if it had fillings.

Like other mediums, Phoebe exerted a power over objects, which in her presence changed not only their places but also density. Sometimes a puddle of semi-transparent liquid would remain where a sculpted console had once been, while a glass of water standing in front of Phoebe at the start of the evening would transmute into a brass paperweight. Things and even people often disappeared from the parlour during a séance. Miriam would later recover the lost objects in distant rooms or rouse the spiritualists put to sleep beside them.

The inhabitants of Providence never tired of accounts of utensils rising into the air at the slightest gesture from the medium's hand, hovering at eye level, suddenly shooting up to hit the ceiling, then dropping onto the knees of the stunned guests. Spoons, forks, book rests would expand in length, then shrink again, twist and turn like a grass snake meandering on a woodland path. Under the hostess's stare, knives would bend, knick-knacks shatter, frames bulge causing the pictures to slip out, teacups crack drenching the lace tablecloths. Shawls fluttering above the table tied themselves in impossible knots. Cigars hanging in the air lit themselves from an invisible match. The phenomenon of apports — transpositions, in other words — reached such a scale in the second year of Phoebe's mediumistic activity that even massive items of furniture, unable to stay in one place, would shift towards their mistress as she sat in a deep trance. The more tired she felt, the more aggressively they behaved. Clocks or watches dozing in the spiritualists' pockets brought fresh surprises, running too fast or too slow, as if not wound for ages. Only a non-participant in a séance could therefore estimate its length. After the first evenings, Phoebe removed the barometer from the wall so that what showed on its face wouldn't distract her guests.

The olfactory sensations accompanying the apports and transformations were so unusual that Phoebe's neighbour, the poet Sarah Helen Whitman, dedicated a poem to them titled "Euphoric Scents of the Beyond," telling of a sandalwood fragrance unknown to the East Coast, of a lion shut in a cage and of spices used in Indian cuisine. Literary historians blame Whitman's fascination with Spiritualism for her conflicts with Edgar Allan Poe, which on the day before their planned wedding on 25 December 1848 led to their permanent separation. Following this unhappy event, the poet formed no other attachment. For the rest of her life, on Phoebe's persuasion, she wore a coffin-shaped charm round her neck, meant to facilitate contact with the Other Side. The séances she conducted never matched

Phoebe's in spectacular effects, yet the spirits of dead bards summoned from the Beyond no doubt whispered a thing or two in the ear of the artist seeking inspiration.

The most devoted spiritualists claimed every séance provided them with a glimmer of confidence that they knew how the world functions. For such moments they were ready to give a lot.

Although so different from her imitators, Phoebe observed many of the rules that would later become de rigueur for a successful séance. For instance, she didn't allow spirits to be subjected to provocative questions. She preferred not to aggravate the Beyond, just in case. Deep in her soul she probably suspected good relations with the Other Side might facilitate her understanding of This One. Not all phantoms appreciated the medium's discretion. Some of the most intractable were spirits of former policemen, still intent on imposing on the spiritualists long-forgotten regulations.

Like her successors, Phoebe sometimes mistook the living for the dead. She would excuse such blunders by explaining her confusion when encountering citizens of Providence bursting with health yet destined — of this she had no doubt — for an early death. Many spirits were in much better shape than they. The absence of order between the worlds inclined her to conjecture that reality was merely a product of human imagination. Plagued by such thoughts, she once stabbed her thumb during a séance with a hatpin as "a test." The incident was recalled many years later when Phoebe's disappearance supplied fuel for gossip about the self-destructive tendencies of mediums.

BIRDS

It all started during an evening at the Civins', when a parrot unexpectedly succumbed to the magic of Phoebe's voice as if she were expert in hypnosis, not mediation between the Worlds. Hardly had Phoebe intoned the séance's opening hymn when the bird fell lifeless from its perch. Strenuous efforts from the hosts were required to bring it round. Not long afterwards, a canary belonging to her neighbours on Transit Street paid for her visit with its life. Following this event, she no longer risked contacts with birds. She explained her effect on them as the result of the fluids she emitted. These were further proof she was a genuine medium.

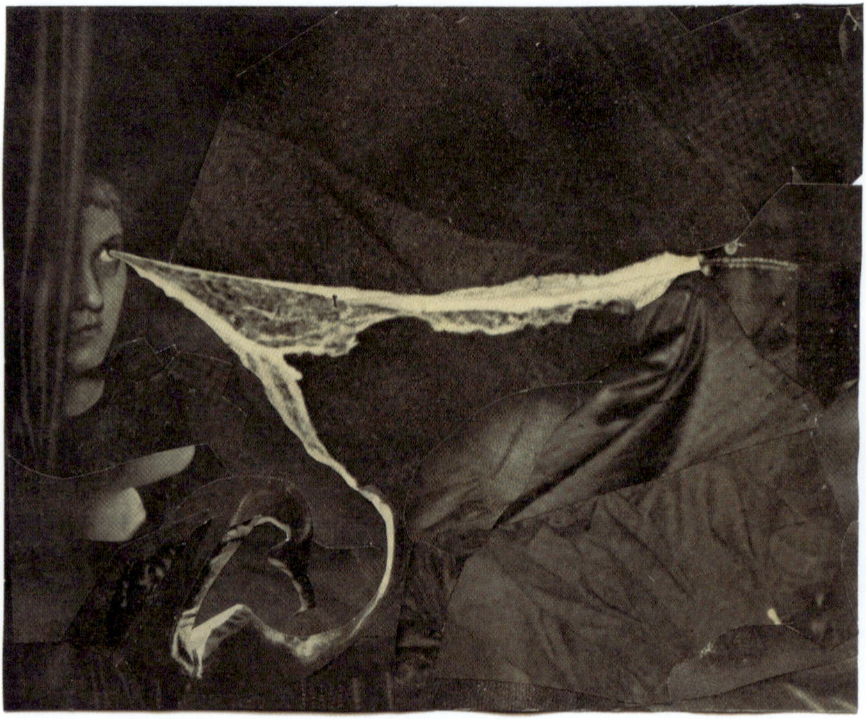

PHOEBE'S MAGNETIC STARE

Her followers believed with equal devotion in animal magnetism. They were ready to swear that positive energy emanates from the right hand and negative energy from the left, while current flows between them. And that moving the palm of a hand over the length of the body, without touching it, cures illnesses. And that animal magnetism has the power to disarm opponents — all it takes is to stare at them intently, trying not to blink, for them to turn away and leave the room.

Phoebe practised this method so assiduously that during one of her séances the dentures of a lady ill-disposed towards her fell out in full view of the assembled guests. One glance at a photograph of Phoebe Hicks was enough to cease being surprised by the devastations wrought by her stare.

CHAIRS

Like the mediums that succeeded her, Phoebe preferred to sit on wooden or wickerwork chairs. And though their hardness did not aid concentration, soft seats entailed even greater dangers since the aura of spirits from previous séances permeates the upholstery and puts fresh arrivals off their visitations. The next generation of mediums received this knowledge from tales circulating in Providence about the séances held in Phoebe's house. She herself acquired it — like everything else — by accident. At the beginning of her career she would sit in her grandmother's soft chair with its violet plush cover. But one evening someone mistakenly drew up a small wicker armchair that had been standing in the corner. That night the medium and her guests were unable to fend off the phantoms infiltrating through every crack in the floorboards until dawn. As if previously kept at arm's length, they now rushed headlong at the living, ready to spend considerably longer time with them than dictated by the etiquette governing relations between the Worlds. The second and third experiments with the wicker chair produced similar results, thereby revealing the secret of a successful séance. Or rather one of the secrets.

FULL MOON

Phoebe Hicks was a discreet person. She strove, for instance, to conceal the fact that the full moon affected her already shaky equilibrium. And that for several nights beforehand she felt anxious and found it harder than usual to concentrate in the ring formed of joined hands. Covering the windows made no difference. Even in foul weather she sensed the sinister orb lurking behind the clouds. Her most loyal devotees knew that once a month this person, relatively rational in the morning, would, as darkness fell, resemble an apparition transported from the Other Side. She would mope about the house — contorted like all the houses in this town — talk to herself, sing long forgotten songs, trip up shadows. Make sure no vampires had invaded her spirit world. On this night alone the kinks in the floorboards threatened downfall and a rude awakening from her moonstruck semi-existence. It may have been pure chance her poisoning by the clam fritter coincided with a full moon, or maybe not.

PHOEBE HICKS'S PECULIAR HABITS

Compared to other female residents of Providence, Phoebe Hicks had baffling habits. For example, she used to hand her acquaintances fragments of a china jug or basin to ascertain later whether they still fitted together. If they did — it was a sign of true friendship between herself and the recipient of the broken vessel. If not — she ended all contact.

Malicious tongues claimed she never ate anything with so much relish as the vision-inducing mushrooms growing in the Vermont woods. And that she drank only blue-coloured beverages. These rumours, though, were unfounded and meant to prove the medium's eccentricity. As if what she ate and drank had any significance.

Vain female participants in the séances complained her well-to-do house was devoid of mirrors. Such absence was striking when compared to other interiors — where dusty knick-knacks, lamps, and stuffed birds in bell jars inspected themselves in countless crystal looking-glasses. Phoebe did not dwell for long on this matter, just muttered something about professional integrity : she did not wish to take short-cuts and read off the mirrors' surfaces the past and future histories of her guests, to her as clear as day.

One more trait distinguished her from other citizens of Providence. By force of will she could transport herself to another place, usually to a plantation in the South, from where it seems her family originated. The few witnesses — whose accounts cannot be entirely trusted — claimed that in such moments her figure would gradually fade, like a spectre formed of plasma.

AIRING THE HOUSE

The female descendants of well-to-do New England families never ceased to be amazed at Phoebe's lifestyle. Only one of her activities gained their approval : the constant airing of her house through the wide-open doors and windows overlooking Benefit Street. "Phoebe Hicks's madness does have its limits," they whispered amongst themselves. "At least she cares about health and fresh air!" How surprised they would have been to learn it wasn't about air. With energy worthy of a better cause, Phoebe was trying to rid the house of spirits lingering within. Atlantic breezes were to chase from the parlour phantoms refusing after a séance to return to the Beyond. It was a battle doomed to failure, but that's another story.

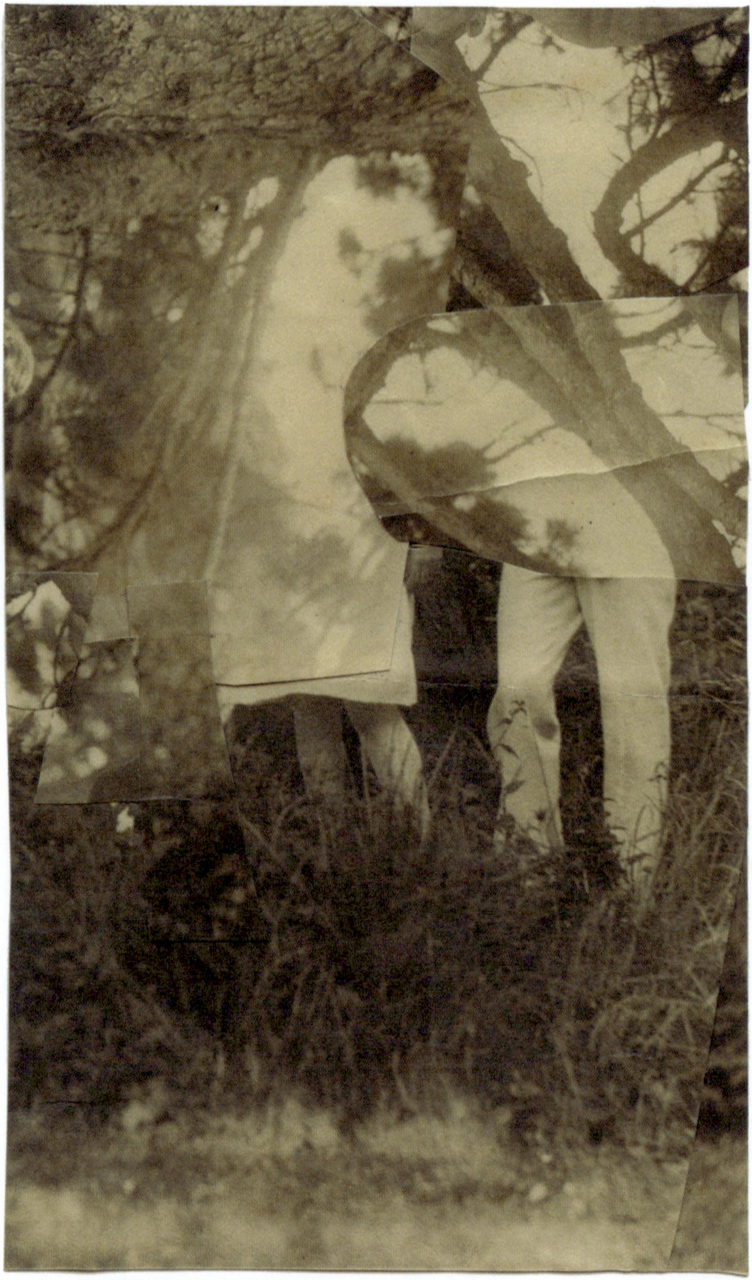

THREE ISLANDS

Phoebe's eccentricity revealed itself, among other things, in her habit of materializing phantoms from the three islands lying off the Providence coast : Nantucket, Block Island and Martha's Vineyard. It was of no concern of hers that none of the assembled spiritualists had any truck with the ghosts of dead fishermen, most regarded the time spent with them as wasted. She pretended not to notice their ire when yet another figure dripping with salt water emerged from behind a curtain. Her attachment to the islands' picturesque landscapes was believed to explain her weakness for the inhabitants. One has to admit the disgruntled spiritualists had a point : the new arrivals had nothing interesting to say.

SICKNESS

Phoebe Hicks sometimes blamed her new choice of occupation on the pain caused by spirits storming her head. The ache would migrate from above one eye to above the other, throbbing beneath her tortured skull as though the phantoms were jostling for space. Only a séance would free her poor head from the uninvited guests. Waking in the early hours, hearing the roar in her temples and feeling the weight of the world on her chest, Phoebe knew the only release would be to listen to the ghosts.

It's not inconceivable that the circumstances that drove her onto the mediumistic path contributed to the emergence of popular theories which perceived disease or nervous shock as a source of extraordinary powers. Almost all mediums suffered from a great variety of ailments ranging from epileptic fits and labyrinthitis to what malicious commentators called hysteria. Medics favourably disposed towards contacts with spirits saw disease as a means of purifying the soul and preparing it for unusual encounters. The idea that the source of such theories lay in Phoebe's poisoning by a clam fritter may seem exaggerated, yet when it comes to Spiritualism it's hard to exaggerate.

SOMETHING THAT MIGHT BE CALLED HYSTERIA

From the time of her disastrous poisoning, Phoebe was thus aware of the presence of spirits placing their spent earthly destinies in her hands. She felt their physical weight on her shoulders, breath on the nape of her neck. With time she grew accustomed to this condition and even began to regard it as normal. Her daytime appearance and behaviour were no different from before the poisoning. Only during séances did she become a different person. Internally unyoked, she ceased to be an old maid fettered by a corset, caring for a cat, which — like her — was unable to stomach the fruits of the sea. Her pale, waxen complexion and glassy stare signalled she was in the sway of visions. There was no way back then. The person so rational during the day would hover for hours on the brink of what some might call — hysteria.

A few ill-disposed doctors claimed that Spiritualism was no more than a safety valve for madness and old-maidenhood, that participation in séances was conducive to hallucinations, that the fashion for table turning, spreading at dizzying speeds, was responsible for madhouses bursting at the seams, that instead of a parlour with its round table a more fitting place for mediums was a hospital isolation ward. Such over-the-top theories later led to the new type of mental illness being designated "mediomania." Behind the doctors' malice stood chiefly a fear of emancipation, as more and more women rejected the social roles ascribed to them in favour of spirits with a democratic disposition.

Ladies participating in séances of fraudulent mediums and succumbing to the extramundane atmosphere were sometimes unable to restrain their own hands rising above the round table towards objects arrayed in the air. The string of dreamers would observe — with pounding hearts — hovering trumpets, garlands of flowers and tiny bells ringing with angelic voices. A shiver would pass through the joined hands as the slender fingers of a guest's recently deceased wife materialised beside them. In the flickering candlelight a white form would be clearly visible against the claret drape, and then suddenly disintegrate. Not for long though, since it quickly reappeared on the lap of the master of the house. Even the most dissolute of female spiritualists deemed this position too forward. Sometimes, in the total darkness, a face radiating with a strange glow would effloresce by a sceptic's ear and whisper a suggestive word. No sooner was the sceptic ready to convert disbelief into ardent faith when the apparition vanished as if behind a dark veil. The slight rustle of garments signalled to those sitting nearest that it was part of a larger whole. Bolder participants occasionally dared to touch the spirit. The corset tangible beneath its robe convinced them the stranger from beyond the grave remained bound to this world by old habits. Discovering no corset released emotions of quite a different nature. Male members of the audience eagerly went over to the new religion.

The phantoms often played tricks. For instance, they might conjure out of Nothingness a flower in a pot, which then proved impossible to dematerialise, and so had to wait until the next séance to return home. Or freshly cut roses would materialise and ascend immediately to the level of the assembled guests' noses so they could relish the heavenly scent. Experienced participants knew the sooner they took advantage of the opportunity the better, since many mediums had a habit of devouring the products they materialised. Before the flowers had their brief sojourn on earth end and disappeared into the mouth exhausted by frequent emissions of ectoplasm, one of the sitters would have enunciated in a solemn voice their Latin names. Victorian exactitude made itself felt in unforeseen moments.

Sometimes, for the sake of a dubious idea of fun, spirits would undo unmarried women's shoes and force them onto the swollen feet of a pastor or banker. Sometimes, following such sport, the shoes vanished for good. Certain disappearances brought an end to the careers of imposters. Such was the case of a resident of Boston's Beacon Hill, regarded in some circles as one of the few genuine mediums. When, during a particularly theatrical séance, a few sceptics rushed behind the curtain — where Miss C. was supposedly sitting in a trance and, in case of anything untoward, tightly bound — all they found were an empty chair and a rope lying on the floor. At this very moment a luminous figure from the Beyond, strangely resembling the medium in height and gait, hastily faded in the dark behind an invisible door. For a while the sound of a guitar and tambourine continued to resound in the air, but soon it too fell silent.

Phoebe Hicks never denied the occurrence of such cases. Compared to them, her séances gained all the more credibility. While other go-betweens with the next world performed a comedy of gyrating tables and meaningful raps, she wasted no time on the fledgling stage of Spiritualism. Having performed

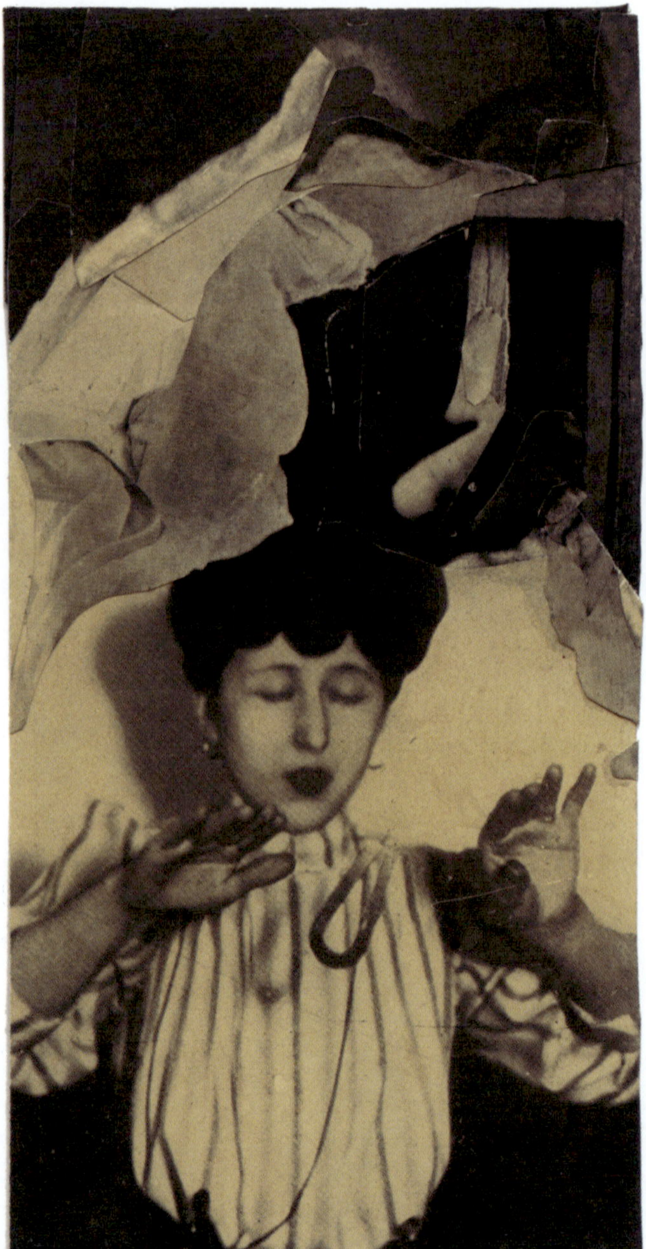

materialisations long before they became the crux of a successful evening, she showed understanding whenever a spirit preferred to make its presence known discreetly — solely by its fragrance or a tremor in the air. In contrast to her impatient successors, she remembered not to disturb persons who had only recently gone over. She knew they needed time to find their bearings in an entirely new situation. With a consistency unknown to other mediums, she liked most to import apparitions who had chosen for eternity the age of thirty and three. The ideal moment — when physical maturity is equal to the spiritual, when Phoebe experienced her revelation, and which had already inscribed itself before into human history.

Various well-known characters summoned from the Other Side manifested themselves through mediums that came after Phoebe — and were especially active during the Civil War when so many people tried to establish contact with deceased loved ones. Sometimes, by means of the medium's fragile fingers, Mozart or Beethoven played music composed beyond the grave. Phantoms wanting to make fun of spiritualist expectations put inappropriate words into the mouths of refined women, prompting curses, vulgar expressions, ambiguous gestures. Mediums were made to slurp whisky from a bottle, spit on the carpet, tell bawdy jokes. The spiritualists sat petrified, convinced the obscenities falling from the lady's mouth were proof of her contact with the other world. Few suspected the medium of wishing to amuse herself by entering with impunity roles inaccessible to her in waking life. Occasionally someone joined in the game, responding in equally unparliamentary language.

Phoebe guaranteed more cultured evenings. She did not impersonate pirates, criminals or demimondaines. Nor did she alter the pitch of her voice, make aggressive movements, or speeches in unknown tongues. She did not use a planchette, the small board with pencil attached that when held by the medium recorded on paper communiqués from the Beyond. She was cautious towards the "miracle" of automatic writing. She strove not to expose her guests to unpleasant encounters, happening so frequently elsewhere that Spiritualism was regarded in some circles as a rapidly spreading contagion. In other houses, heavy objects would fall or parts of the medium's wardrobe drift down onto the assembly. To the ladies' horror, live eels became entangled in their impeccable coiffures. As proof that gardens in the Beyond differed little from the garden plots of Providence's middle-class citizens, the heads of such unfortunates were bombarded with flowers torn up by the roots and covered in fresh soil. Chairs unexpectedly broke. Materialised figures ruffled participants' hair, tugged at their ears and noses, kicked them in the calves, stole their purses and jewellery, struggled to unhook ladies' dresses, cut out holes in gentlemen's frock coats, sprinkled with ash, sprayed with nauseous scent, or sometimes ordinary pitch. They overturned furniture, pulled down drapes, blew out weakly burning lamps, and left behind gifts of a dubious nature : bits of white gauze or an inflatable rubber glove that a moment earlier had been stroking the spiritualists' faces. Occasionally, the phantoms of ethereal ladies offered locks of hair or scraps of dresses to enamoured gentlemen.

In Phoebe's house such things did not occur. While the characters she materialised did tend to be boring or eccentric, they were never dangerous. Phoebe also never sat — like other mediums — tied to a chair and separated by a heavy drape from the rest of the room. She was not amused by circus tricks, such as freeing herself from bonds, climbing onto a chair and displaying her head, wrapped in gauze, through a hole in the curtain. Nor waving before the noses of guests a hand smeared with glow-in-the-dark paint, nor concealing under her dress wires which in the culminating moment of the séance set in motion the table that had been peacefully dormant on its castored legs.

She did not deny that other mediums took advantage of their guests' gullibility. In attempting to obliterate any resemblance between the ghostly countenances and the guide to the other side frozen in a trance behind the curtain, they would put on wigs beneath their tulle veils. In preparing to materialise a whole form, they would daub a white silk robe in phosphorescent paint. In trying to achieve an extramundane look, they would rub their lips with wax and administer eye drops that dilated the pupils. They perfected the art of putting their guests in such a peculiar state of mind they were ready to believe anything. As Phoebe didn't have to do this, she wasn't threatened with being unmasked : the sudden throwing back of the curtain to reveal to the assembled eyes an empty chair, while the medium disguised as a phantom blew the breath of the Beyond into the spiritualists' hair. In her parlour it was pointless to wait for the appearance of waxen spectral hands or mandolins and accordions whirling in the air, so popular at other séances. Why didn't she resort to trickery to inflame the senses and imagination? Maybe she had no need to pull the wool over her followers' eyes. Or had such belief in her own charisma she didn't want others to be distracted by little bells, disembodied hands, or fragments of her wardrobe falling from the ceiling.

WHOSE TRANCE?

Perhaps it was not Phoebe who slipped into a trance, but the séance participants? Perhaps she just controlled with calculated calm how the others shut their eyes, how their hands trembled, how the tears dropped onto the wine-coloured cloth? Maybe her aim was to regale the inhabitants of Providence with strong emotions? And because she couldn't do it any other way, she opted for trickery. Pure conjecture, but not so improbable.

Few realised Phoebe was more than a go-between for the Beyond. Well acquainted over the years with human nature, she would assume the role of psychoanalyst *avant la lettre*. Before darkness descended along with the start of the séance, she would patiently hear out her clients, rarely interrupting with a question or comment. Perhaps — not unlike the fraudulent mediums — she took advantage of a chance to acquire useful information. It seems something more was at stake. Like Freud later, she was fascinated by other people's accounts of missed opportunities, squandered potentials, alternative versions of life that wielded boundless power over the imagination. This too distinguished her from other mediums.

HEAD OF THE COUCH

In her new life, the thing Phoebe most valued was that her thoughts — up until then so restless — now revolved around one issue : whether the next séance would be just as successful as the last. Such a clearly formulated goal brought inner peace. Wishing to share with others her simple discovery about how to make sense of life, she even contemplated changing her profession. She imagined herself sitting in a comfortable armchair at the head of a couch on which a patient lay relaxing. She listens attentively and then gives her advice — which is always the same : they should devote themselves to some mission provided it is done absolutely. Apparently she came quite close to making the change, but was dissuaded by the obtrusive materialisations of a German-speaking boy who would reiterate with a persistence worthy of a better cause that this particular career had been assigned to him. The toddler kept appearing at the most inappropriate moments until she promised to drop the idea. The visits were so exhausting she never investigated why he had left behind his earthly shell in Europe to plague as a luminous phantasm this Atlantic town.

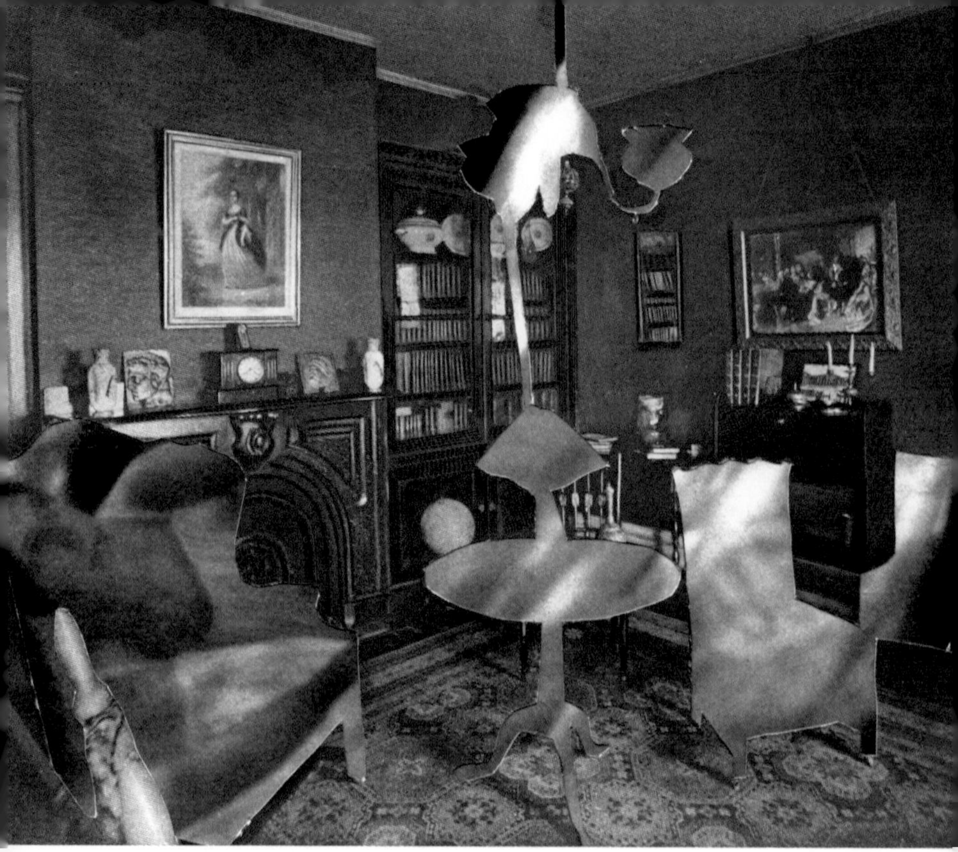

THE HOUSES' FATIGUE

And now a few words about the town without which there would have been no Phoebe and no séances, without which the spirits would have been condemned to remain forever on the Other Side. Providence is the capital of Rhode Island — the smallest state in the union, an important hub of New England, the European part of America.

All its streets give the impression of being side streets, so limited is the traffic on them and so insignificant the role they seem to play in the life of the town. They are like old stage sets stored in a props room, not used for years, but from behind which ghosts of past productions might peep at any moment. The disorientated pedestrian will rarely stray this way, overawed by the crushing atmosphere of provincial banality. This type of difficult-to-define atmosphere no doubt had its effect on the imagination of Phoebe Hicks.

Just as the town had formed her, so she had an influence upon the town. Her séances were rightly seen as the source of changes beginning to affect the houses. For the houses of Providence are bursting at the seams. Walls stretch and bulge under the impact of the spirits that inhabit them, of vapours rising from once living matter, of unfinished conversations hanging in the air. Interrupted sentences and questions without answers grow heavier and heavier with time, bloated like dry bread rolls soaking up water. The walls of especially haunted houses are almost oval. Inhabitants of neighbouring towns laugh at Providence and long into the night discuss the superiority of straight lines over crooked. The uncouth nature of the citizens of Johnston, Warwick or Pawtucket keeps them from inquiring into the cause of the swelling walls. Their views have no effect on the habits of the spirits, of course. What's more, some ghosts, bored by their sojourn in the Beyond, seem to derive a particular pleasure from altering the shapes of the walls. It's enough to walk down Benefit Street in the late afternoon, when the setting sun casts shadows of gas lanterns against distended façades, emphasising their absurd forms, to grasp the scale of the disturbing transformations.

Houses in Providence also have wrinkles. No one speaks openly of the connection between the frequency of the séances conducted within them and the pace of their ageing. It's an open secret that the shortest séance transforms even quite new façades beyond recognition — like a sleepless night can add years to a human face. From the degree to which the paint is cracked or walls are crooked, from the feeling that a ceiling is about to cave in, connoisseurs can tell how often the occupants succumb to their addiction of communing with spirits. As a matter of fact, you don't have to be a great specialist to observe the symptoms. It's enough to be born in Providence, or stay there a little while, to see the house fatigue as clear as day.

THE ANIMALS

There's no way to avoid the question of the animals. Many residents of Providence have a real obsession with them. Not that there are more animals than in neighbouring towns, or they're more obtrusive or more visible than, say, in Fall River, or Pawtucket. There are just as many skunks, squirrels, foxes, opossums, mice, coyotes, rats, hares, raccoons, feral cats and birds of prey as in other New England harbour towns. And yet the local residents perceive them differently . . . Citizens of Providence can hold forth for hours about their nocturnal encounter with a rat chased by a cat darting past in the light of a street lamp, or the eyes of a squirrel surprised by the sudden swoop of a hawk. Such accounts reflect no love for the rat or squirrel. If a storyteller betrays a note of sympathy, it's more likely directed at the predator than the prey. As if the inhabitants, crushed by the presence of the spirits, sought in its strength the fulfilment of their own dreams of power. As if, accustomed to giving way to shadows, they let themselves be hypnotized by outstretched wings, lightning-swift movements, the aggressive shape of a beak. As if, without admitting it, they identified more with the squirrel than the hawk. And, finally, pushing the thought deep into their unconscious, as if they felt relieved they were not the object of an attack.

Another factor in the hysteria surrounding animals is surely the omnipresence of the colonial architecture, which bestows a special aura on every scurrying mouse or bird of prey circling above a squirrel. The case of Timothy O'Neill, Phoebe's neighbour from Sheldon Street, was a direct result of the atmosphere

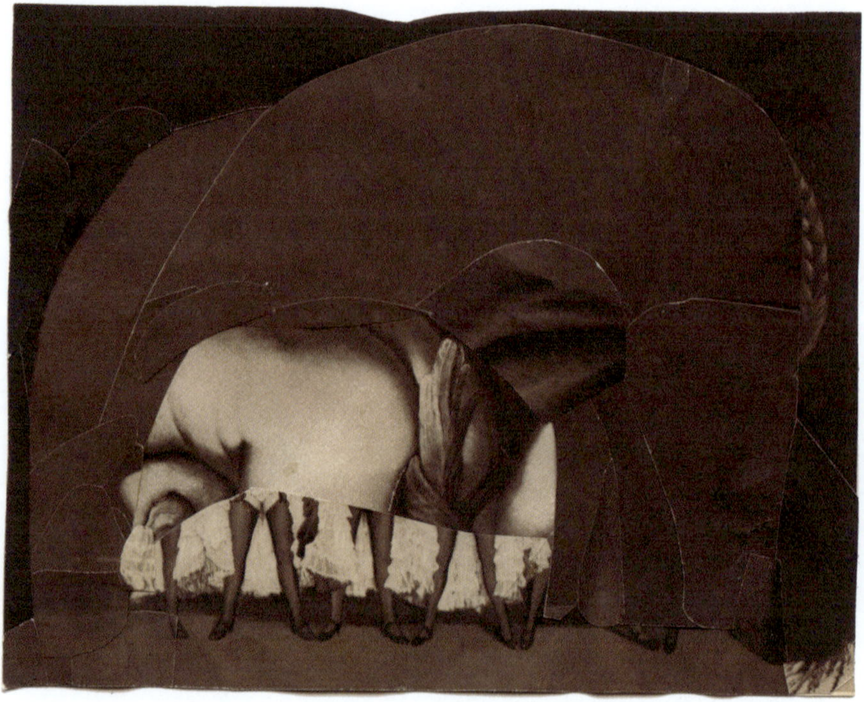

created by Providence's houses. Suffering from an odd affliction, he joined the séances in the hope they might rid him of his obsession. Day and night he was plagued by the idea that some small animal whose name he did not know had jumped on his back. Timothy O'Neill cared less and less about his work at the bank and spent less and less time relaxing with his family in the garden, becoming utterly obsessed with how to catch his tormentor, which always vanished at the last moment, leaving him with scratches on his back and a sense of defeat.

Although Phoebe lived her own life, impenetrable to others, the attention she paid to animals — of this world and the next — bound her to the inhabitants of the magic town. Let's take the case of the whalebone. By the fireplace in the Thomsons' drawing room on Williams Street stood a whale vertebra which served as a seat, the whale having been caught — it so happened — in the year Phoebe was born. Guests loved to sit on it. Phoebe alone refused every time she was offered the place of honour. Something about the bone revolted her. Fear of the lack of back support. Concern that her dress might get crumpled and ash soil the hem. Dislike of the ocean, incomprehensible for a coastal inhabitant. Nausea at the thought of her own bone being so close to another's. The thought of eating ox tongue aroused a similar revulsion. Never ever would she take it into her mouth! She would sooner swallow tripe, only to bring it up again later discreetly into the flowery washbasin. The prospect of ox tongue in her mouth, tongue against tongue, the idea of the moribund yet still bodily muscle touching her own sticky, pulsating tongue covered in volcanoes and mountain passes, made her stomach heave.

The encounter between her bone and the bone of the whale, dead for over thirty years, was not the only thing that Phoebe found disagreeable. She was also disturbed by the unexplained sympathy she felt for the creature which — of this she was sure — had fallen victim to a harpooner before it had fully tasted the enchantments of life.

The omnipresence of spirits in Providence explains the success of Phoebe's séances. It is true that other towns also have their ghosts — nowhere, however, are they so noisy and restless. So many phantoms live in Providence they fill every nook and cranny. Saturated with their breath, the air grows oppressive and causes headaches. You don't so much walk down the streets as fight your way through invisible throngs. At night, the phantoms moan as if united by a common cause for which they've come to seek redress. Little bands of girls in white dresses hover above the pavement and then, whispering and giggling, vanish behind the gate of a neglected mansion. High-spirited ghosts blow hot wind into the hair of idle strollers, giving the lie to the belief it's always cold in the Beyond. Hysterical laughter reverberates through the air, reaches its peak after thirty seconds or so and suddenly falls silent. Then, for a while, the madness dissipates from the streets, only to return in the shape of spectral old women who, having spent their whole lives in the harbour town, cannot get used to their new home. They roam the provincial squares — unkempt, wretched, speechless, quite different from the spirits of their beautiful neighbours who passed away in their youth.

Not all Providence's phantoms are ephemeral. Some are corporeal, even corpulent. They have pimply faces and dirty fingernails, and reek at times of underwear seldom changed. Contact with them is unpleasant — like touching a sticky, unwashed hand. Not distinguished by the usual runniness of putrid matter, or the chilly aura of the tomb, their unearthly nature is given away by their style, so different from what characterized them in life! Old bigots return from the Beyond in lace ball gowns with enhanced waistlines and plunging necklines, coquettish outmoded beauty spots affixed to their cheeks, flowers and ribbons woven into their hair, while they fan themselves with fingers laden with rings, cast provocative glances, and — if permitted to stay longer — make suggestive gestures. They smoke pipes of tobacco with a strong nauseating aroma. The smell alone evokes rotting flesh, before the dead assume their ghostly forms. Sometimes they carry balloons and try to mount them in moments of heightened debauchery, seemingly half-demented, just as they did before death, except now their madness is of a different order.

The citizens of Providence associate the presence of phantoms with the presence of women. Male spirits rarely interfere in the affairs of the living — out of habit or discretion spending most of their time in the harbour, where few mortals venture after dusk. They relish the sea air, compare the vestiges of their tattoos and drink something that resembles beer, which obviously is not beer, but drinking too is a mere simulation of a once oft-repeated activity. They usually remain silent in their total absorption, thus sparing the living the most unpleasant auditory sensations produced by intercourse with the Beyond.

Come morning, many ghosts sink below ground, yet memories of the night prevent the living from fully enjoying the sunlight. Few bold adventurers dare to steal down the streets of Providence at daybreak. Pale countenances, now dispossessed of their bodies, peer out from everywhere, as if making the most of the final moments before the light banishes them temporarily. They whisper, shout, jostle, shove past one another, and grab the

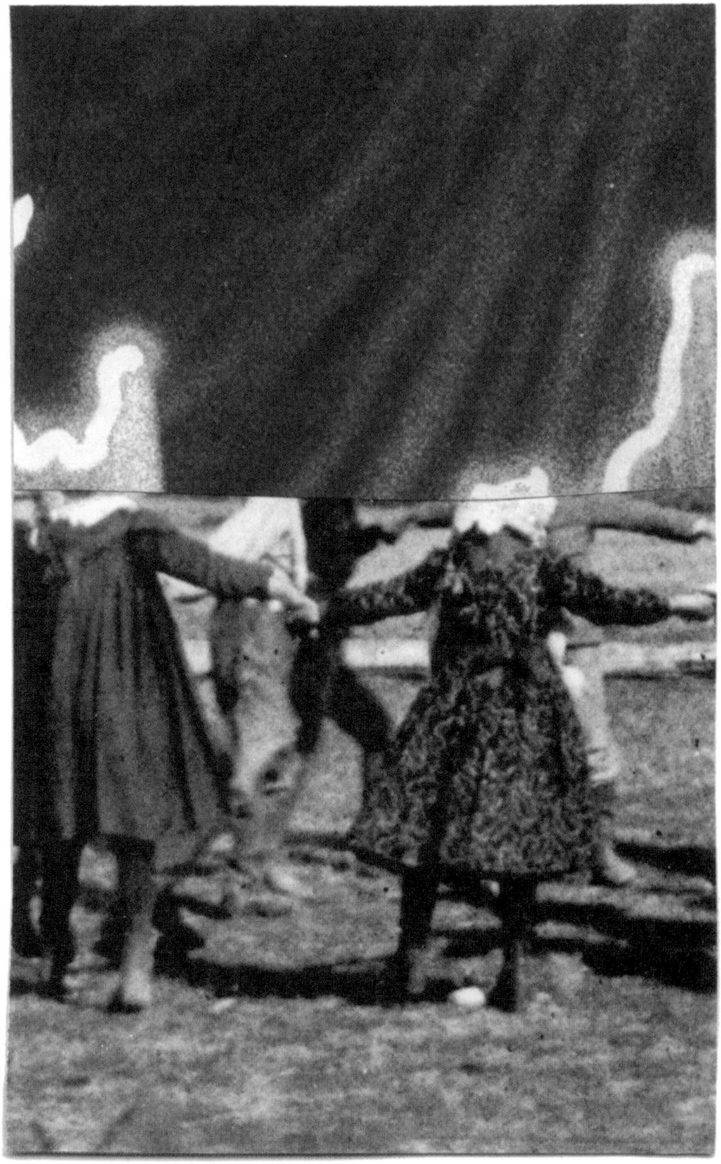

trouser-legs or skirt-hems of infrequent passers-by. Workers tell of such encounters as they hurry to their workplaces, fighting their way across the haunted town. Several women have lost their senses walking down Waterman Street at dawn. Most families have someone in a mental institution. Lunacy afflicts New England more than other parts of America — doctors rightly forbid patients with nervous dispositions to leave their homes. Only around noon is it relatively safe to brave this town of pitfalls alone. At any other time the spirits are able to sense a potential victim some distance away, and it's rare for a sensitive walker not to succumb to an attack of madness or depression on returning from a stroll.

SPIRITS LIKE TO JOIN IN MEDIAS RES

Why spirits should derive pleasure from driving mortals crazy — it's hard to make out. There's no point repeating the dubious theories circulating on the subject. Instead, several reasons why phantoms have taken a liking to New England, and especially to the town of Providence, deserve mention.

First, noises issue from the ground, as if the dead were changing positions in which they've been lying for too long, or even intended to temporarily abandon their graves. The phenomenon has been ascribed to the peculiar geology of the terrain, confirmed by scientific research. But anyone who lives in Providence knows it's better to treat science with caution.

Second, the proximity of the ocean sometimes prompts a sea-breeze smelling of seaweed to rush through the narrow streets. Though bringing relief on summer afternoons, it also arouses anxiety and a longing for something intimate yet elusive. This obsessive feeling is enough for the more delicate inhabitants to suffer from life-long melancholy. The breeze is also an omen of things invisible which, if they don't materialise quickly enough, provide fuel for visions. And it is precisely such visions, some would claim, that attract spirits who like to join narratives in medias res.

Third, the coastal wind — more prevalent than elsewhere — drives mists onto the town that resemble the clouds of plasma visible in séance photographs. Apart from Phoebe Hicks's poisoning by the clam, the flourishing of séances owed much to the maritime climate.

ANOMALIES

Anomalies in the weather, like all deviations from the norm, put spirits in an excellent mood. Snowstorms in April, spring temperatures in mid-February, hurricanes, floods, blasts of fantasy in respectable citizens, gusts of folly in ladies cramped by corsets — phantoms lap it all up. Whenever a blizzard blows so hard it breaks a window in someone's home or the pastor of the white Baptist church gets carried away by shockingly frivolous digressions (which he bitterly regrets afterwards), the spectres cackle in the aisles and outshout one another, though their laughter differs somewhat from what we call laughter on Earth. The séance participants asked about the cause of such hilarity. Phoebe's replies were cryptic. She didn't want to divulge the embarrassing truth that spirits take joy in anything disrupting earthly life, which from the perspective of the Beyond seems monotonous in the extreme.

PINK PETALS

For two brief spring weeks the magic town of Providence becomes filled with pinkish-white petals. Torn off the fruit trees, more numerous here than elsewhere, they spiral in mid-air imbued with the ocean scent and warmed by the sun for the first time in the year, before falling to earth and landing in thick layers on streets, gardens, porches and roofs. Distinct from the autumn carnival of colour, the spring madness is short-lived enough to command each day the entire attention of the inhabitants. Perhaps it's this undivided attention that makes the spirits, offended they've suddenly stopped playing the most important role in people's lives, interfere with redoubled energy. The strangest, most sinister intrusions by phantoms into the affairs of the living occur during the spring equinox. In no other season do so many household objects vanish from their customary places. At no other time of year do so many residents leap up in the middle of the night, roused by a heavy visitation from the Beyond. In no other winter, summer or autumn month do so many lunatics end up in hospital possessed by demons. During the April apogee, more patrons than ever knocked on Phoebe's door drowning in the sea of petals, hoping a séance would liberate them from the menace hanging over their heads. In contrast to the sluggish séances held in the autumn, the ones in April were distinguished by a tension unknown in other months, inspired by the participants' belief that anything could happen. It was in April that Phoebe's duel with the spirit of the greatest magician of all time took place.

JOKES

Lost among real and transitory forms, the inhabitants of the magic town no longer recognize who is from this world and who from the next. There is nothing left but to wait until the amorphous individuals begin to tell jokes. If totally hermetic, then it's clear the tellers are visitors from the Other Side. The naivety with which spirits unmask themselves is puzzling. As if they can't resist a good yarn.

Some phantoms seem just as astonished by their sojourn in this world as mortals who observe it. Now and then they compulsively repeat the same words or motions, as if through familiar gestures and sounds trying to prove to themselves they again exist. Their maniacal behaviour makes the living attribute offences to them they've not committed : breaking a window, spreading fire, displacing objects to weird places, shooting furniture or utensils into the air, making superfluous objects appear in houses, the banging of shutters, the sudden opening of locked doors. Spirits attempt to protest against the baseless accusations, yet few among the living notice their protest.

Misunderstandings also arise from phantoms' physicality and the way they look. Desiring to see in them ethereal creatures fashioned from congealed mist, séance participants were invariably amazed when their hands did not sink into a spirit as if into dough but settled on entirely material skin. Hence the rumours about mediums disguised as ghosts. This "nebulous" situation gave some sitters an excuse for impertinent behaviour. New England gentlemen risked outbursts of Phoebe's fury when groping women visiting from beyond the grave.

TWO REALITIES

As long as the two realities existed alongside one another, Phoebe could control the situation. When they started to interpenetrate, she panicked. She was then plagued by optical illusions brought on by — so she believed — spirits to whom she hadn't devoted sufficient attention. For instance, hair pomade would be transformed before her very eyes into whipped cream and land in her coffee, which she'd been intending to drink black. Sometimes hallucinations took on even more aggressive forms. Furniture coming to life, utensils crumbling to dust, liquids evaporating in a split second, flower-stalks standing in a vase stiffening into wood — were among the daily torments of Phoebe Hicks. The lives of frauds were certainly easier. Only trance would deliver her from this intermediate state. Sinking into it reminded her of falling asleep. It calmed her, bringing at the same time fear of bad dreams.

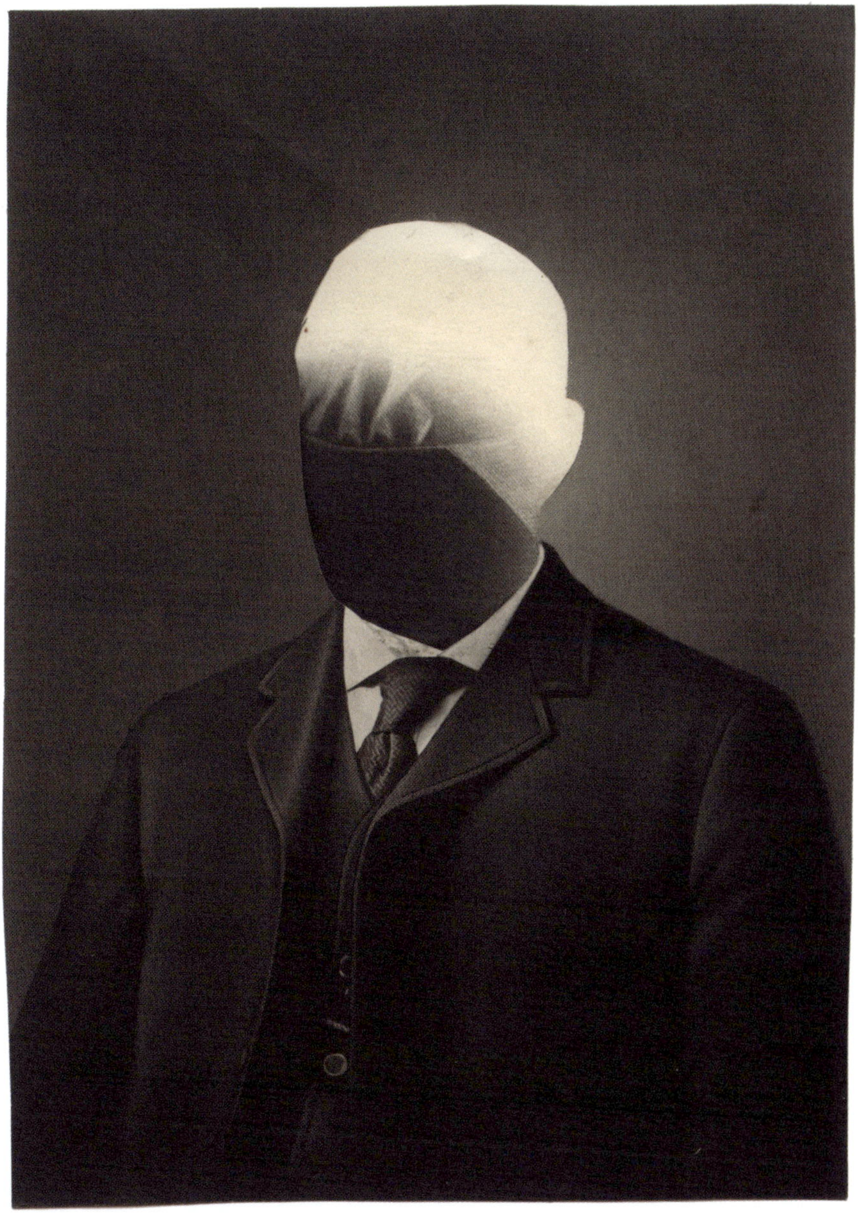

BETRAYED BY A SLIGHT MISHAP

Of all Providence's inhabitants gripped by fantasies of the Beyond, Phoebe alone knew that spirits are not infallible. The same vices and virtues, fears and irrational thoughts someone had in life are retained in the afterlife. A sojourn on the Other Side does not at all imply ascending towards a higher level of consciousness. Spirits are just as much characterized by selective knowledge as the boorish neighbours on Benefit Street. Phoebe quickly understood there are phantoms who mimic the living so well their ghostliness is hard to discern. They are betrayed by a slight mishap testifying to their unearthly nature. Since it is such a rare occurrence, those who have witnessed it refuse to acknowledge what they have seen.

In the whole magic town, only Phoebe spent enough time with ghosts to fully realise their malicious nature. For reasons unknown this trait was ignored by her neighbours harried by spectres. For motives unclear, the living turned a blind eye to spirits toying with human naivety and playing pranks of a dubious class. Providence's inhabitants preferred to pretend they were untouched by the open secret. That so many people ended up in madhouses was taboo. No one mentioned the obvious fact that the town's citizens were always accompanied by their dead day and night, and that the most devastating consequences were from those fractions of a second when mortals caught in the corner of their eye the presence of new arrivals from yonder, taking part in their lives as if nothing had happened. At such moments the boundaries between life and death were completely porous.

Phoebe knew that whether someone went insane depended on what kind of spirit had taken possession of them. The poor wretch might begin to drink, steal, curse, brawl, be afraid of everything, or threaten others with a knife. Suddenly fall ill, start to stutter or develop allergies, become a drug addict, if possessed by the spirit of an opium-eater. There was no way back to the state prior to the visitation. Phoebe shared with no one her knowledge that spirits do not always infiltrate the victim immediately : they lurk initially in the house where a séance was conducted. Bide their time. A whole year might pass before they haunt a member of the household, and not necessarily one who participated in the séance. Sometimes a medium herself succumbs to possession after a first attempt to make contact with the Beyond. She may even on occasion call up spirits many times over and yet seem to remain in her right mind. It takes a while for the people around her to notice that something is odd. At first the changes are insignificant, especially when the spirit has a cheerful disposition. But once a channel is opened, more monsters will stream through.

The truth about Phoebe Hicks therefore waits to be uncovered. It's surprising no one has ever filmed her story. Alain Resnais originally intended to make her the heroine of his *Providence*. Did he give up the idea for lack of adequate information? Because of the disturbing ambiguity of what we do know about her? Or maybe the precursor of New Wave cinema discovered something else, of which no one before had any inkling? Otherwise, how to explain the sudden changes made to the script so late in the day? The fury of the producer, who saw in the director's prevarications only financial loss, is quite understandable. The spirit of Providence that Resnais supposedly sought died along with Phoebe — sealed by the funeral cortège that processed from the Baptist church to Swan Point Cemetery. Why then did he pass over her existence in silence?

Or maybe the mystery surrounding her life stemmed not from contact with disembodied spirits, but from physical relationships with people? Perhaps our ignorance springs from Victorian hypocrisy? Perhaps Phoebe Hicks was above all a beautiful woman conscious of her sexuality? Young mediums used to dress for séances in unbuttoned robes, wearing nothing underneath. In the dark, they let chosen participants touch the earthly forms of emissaries from the Beyond. Did Phoebe also do this? In an era when a woman's hair straying from under her hat could inflame the senses, the erotic atmosphere of the séance was an important engine of their popularity.

Towards the end of the nineteenth century there were even rumours circulating in Providence that a popular medium had fallen pregnant during a séance. The father was alleged to be a pastor renowned for his piety, who later refused to acknowledge the child. Such a scenario was not impossible. After all, a condition for a successful séance was the obscurity, while the hymns sung by the participants would drown out other sounds.

Men, however, were not the most avid participants of spiritualist meetings. Women were much more deeply involved. They comprised Phoebe Hicks's most loyal court, always ready to offer her the warmth of their palms, prevent her gown slipping from her shoulder, ward off the unwelcome advances of the master of a house. The female inhabitants of Providence fell in love with Phoebe, desiring her with a passion forbidden by Victorian morality. Without their affection, her success would never have been so complete.

But Phoebe rejected the amorous advances of both men and women. She repeated *ad nauseam* that she was bound by love of a cosmic nature to a spiritual guide called Oscar. In her trance, she would describe his powerful shoulders and a triangular bald patch on the crown of his head that particularly excited her. She would imagine his fantastic history, which varied from séance to séance. Once Oscar was a New England gentleman, then a gold prospector from California, then another time — the progeny of European aristocrats with a complex genealogical tree. Although he could have endowed many a Providence puritan with a lavish biography, in comparison with the spiritual guides of other mediums — a one-legged thirteenth-century Patagonian acrobat, a Chinese emperor suffering from somnambulism, a confidante of the Sun King sentenced to the block — Oscar was seen as someone whose life had been entirely humdrum.

Whether he was an imaginary figure, invented to discourage Phoebe's ever expanding circle of admirers — it is hard to know. Maybe she once knew someone of that name, maybe read it in a book. In any case, despite his volatile nature, Oscar provoked the dislike of the séance participants, for whom Phoebe was not only the intermediary between them and the Beyond, but above all the object of desire.

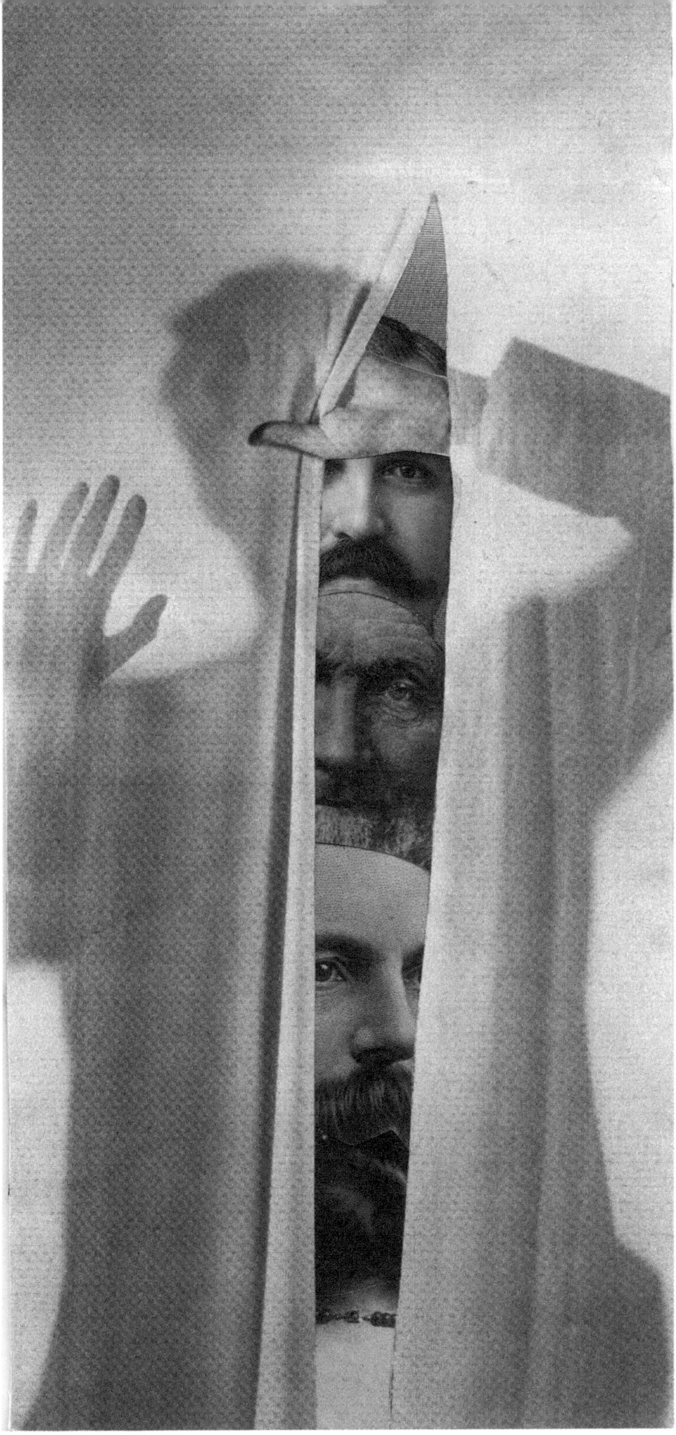

Or maybe Phoebe Hicks was simply an artist? Unaware of her talent, transforming frustration into quasi-fulfilment through contact with non-existent spirits? Perhaps, just as the monster's story, born of unbridled imagination, was the pretext for Mary Shelley to tell of ghouls tormenting us at night, so Oscar was for Phoebe merely a smokescreen? An excuse to withdraw from life, enclose herself in a walnut shell, reject wooers, reduce conversations with neighbours to a minimum, assume an inscrutable expression, forget about reality — erase it, burn its residue, and scatter the ashes at the crossroads? Might this be the secret hidden behind the stony countenance of every medium?

We cannot rule out the possibility, of course, that she was simply a fraud. And yet she conjured up the spirit of Houdini long before the master of underwater escapes was born! This is the one irrefutable fact. So perhaps other manifestations enacted by her were merely fakes intended to pull the wool over the eyes of her naive contemporaries? Maybe she didn't want to fully admit her power? Show she was the only genuine medium?

PERHAPS SHE WAS TIRED OF THE COMPANY OF PEOPLE?

Endeavouring to penetrate the secret of Phoebe Hicks, historians of spiritualism usually begin their investigation with the question why she became a medium. Some apologists think she chose the profession for a prosaic reason : tired of the company of people, she preferred to flee from conversation into monologue. Phoebe's grudging female neighbours, irritated by her stubborn silence whenever they discussed the latest gossip, considered this straightforward reason. The theory might explain her annoying habit of interrupting conversations with a short burst of laughter. It was the signal it was time to part.

If we are to believe what our heroine once said to an insistent journalist immediately after being poisoned by the clam fritter, she had begun to be tormented by a strange, previously unknown sense of invisible beings thronging around her. Whenever she tried to forget this other world, even for a moment, the spirits would press against her legs, suddenly appearing and disappearing before she could establish their age or sex. Sometimes she ran after them, so the sudden manifestations involved the danger of falling and breaking a leg. Her belief that the spirits would derive pleasure from such an accident, along with a vision she'd had of herself lying on a floor in the empty house still ringing with the echo of laughter that had subsided long ago, meant she could never dispel — for the sake of peace of mind — thoughts of New England's dead inhabitants. Exhausted by obtrusive materialisations, Phoebe decided to tame them by involving them in the séance process. The practical side of the medium's personality is something interpreters often overlook.

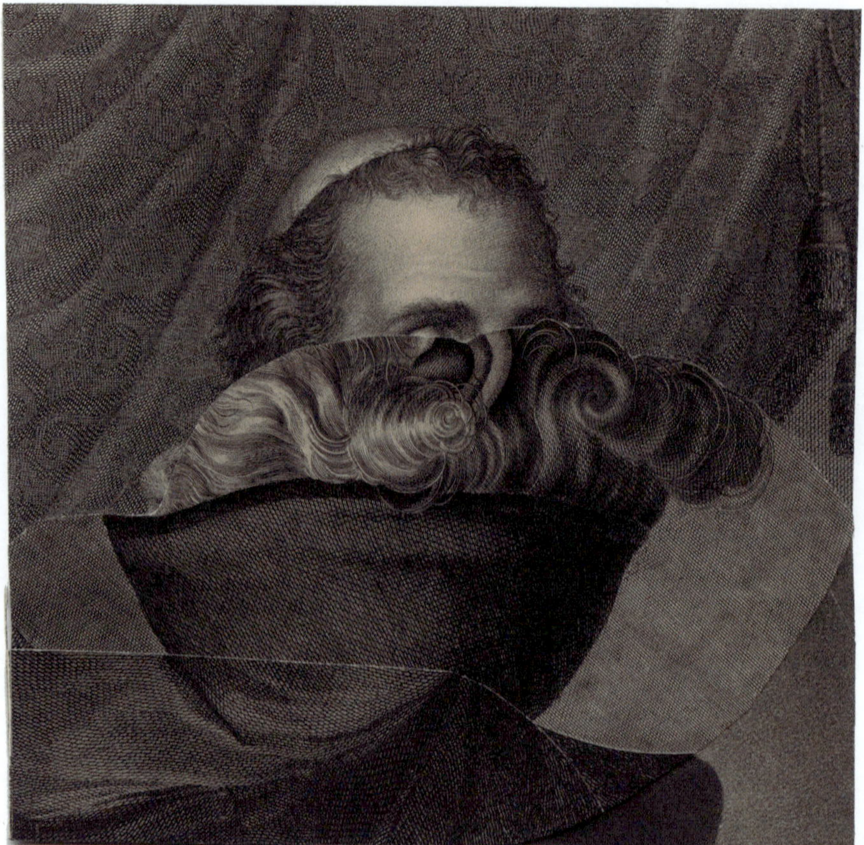

Or maybe she was bored by the banality of conversation and contrived a flight into theatricality? At the beginning at least, the ritual of the séance kept banality at bay, but once the routine had been set, the aura of the first evenings was partly ruined. Yet even then Phoebe's séances were characterized by a certain *je ne sais quoi* that was the envy of other mediums. Did the aura come from her feeling lost? that in her heart of hearts she did not believe in her power? Fiction and reality had become so confused in her mind she was no longer sure of anything. Didn't her sense of humour, which grew so much keener during her career as a medium, suggest a certain aloofness from herself? Chroniclers of Spiritualism are reluctant to admit that her séances afforded participants, apart from the fear and excitement, a good laugh as well. Why such selectivity? Was it a desire to imbue Phoebe's story with an atmosphere of erotic scandal? One has only to leaf through Providence's newspapers published during her heyday to encounter images of a young brunette sitting rigid in trance, her gaze fixed on the snow-covered roofs of wooden houses beyond the window. The slight parting of her robes hints at the nakedness beneath — sometimes implied by the commentary. Though it was something obvious to her contemporaries, never is any mention made of Phoebe's intelligence.

EUROPEAN POSTCARDS

It's a wonder Phoebe's renown never reached Europe. All the more so since Spiritualism was the first movement to hail from the United States. If she'd been born half a century later, European cities would surely have been swamped with post-cards of her likeness. They're not hard to imagine : *en face* close-ups of her expressive countenance looming out of the dark, or shots of her profile emphasising the tightly twisted bun, embellished with a silk appliqué or a sky-blue feather glued to the side. Sometimes a general view : the circle of figures sitting round a table in the glow of an oil lamp — turned up at the photographer's request — as if they were unsure themselves to which world they belonged. Or postcard collages : a miniature Phoebe sprouts from a rosebud, soars over Paris thanks to sketched-in wings, or winks at us from a bottle floating on the waves. Though despite her popularity guaranteed by the cards, Phoebe's truly American gift — the ability to metamorphose — might not have appealed to Europeans. Either way, her story is not only very American but connected to a very specific place. Phoebe Hicks was more strongly bound to the East Coast than any other nineteenth-century personality of comparable fame. The murky back streets of Providence had a more powerful effect on her imagination than California, which is much too sunny for visitors from the Beyond.

AND ONE MORE THING

Human malice made Phoebe's life fuel for the most ridiculous gossip. The absurdity record was broken by one piece of "verified information" circulating after her disappearance, which claimed that as a medium of genius she'd become so fused with the non-material world she'd assumed the shape of an ethereal ball. Providence's windbags kept repeating that her successors owed their fame to the Phoebe-ball moulded during especially difficult séances. The rumour likely had its source in Phoebe's practical method for concentrating the mind, though it remains a mystery how her secret became public knowledge.

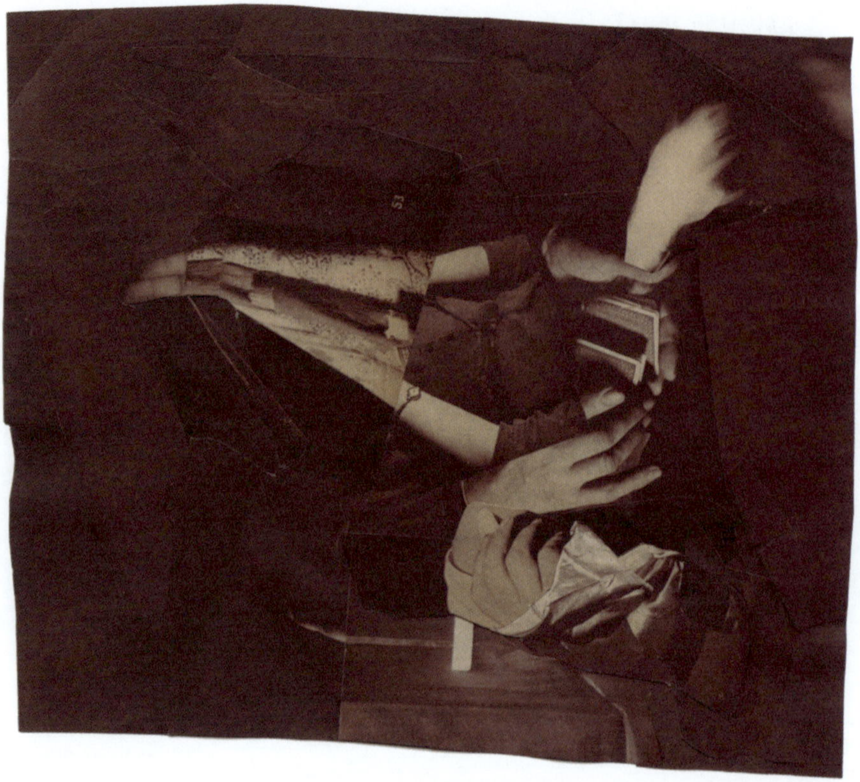

THE UNFINISHED LIFE OF PHOEBE HICKS

On 6 September 18 . . . , on page five of the *Providence Times* under the heading Miscellanea, a notice appeared with the enigmatic title *The Unfinished Life of Phoebe Hicks*. The author — signed by the initials J.T. — maintained that at the end of one of her séances, Phoebe Hicks had dematerialised. She left behind a cat which her neighbours, who'd taken part that evening, adopted until its mistress's return. J.T. expressed the view that the medium's disappearance was linked to the loss of her powers. This interpretation was based on a faith in Phoebe's integrity, which no one publicly ever doubted. No longer capable of further excursions into the Beyond, she preferred to withdraw from the stage than perform a comedy.

Her dematerialisation coincided with several local scandals exposing frauds. An especially dramatic case was that of Mrs C. of Westport, caught pretending to be the ghost of a slave woman from Alabama. Crawling on her knees, her face obscured by a dark mask, the medium was taken unawares by the striking of a sulphur match.

Ten years later, the same newspaper which had covered Phoebe's disappearance and the exposure of Mrs C., reported the record-breaking long life of the cat that had once belonged to Phoebe Hicks, citizen of Providence, and then to Mr and Mrs Howard, residents of Benefit Street. This second notice referred neither to the profession nor to the dematerialisation of the original owner. A third article, supplied with an illustration, was an account of Phoebe's funeral, which took place thirteen years after she vanished from the face of the earth. What happened to the medium in the meantime — remains a mystery to this day.

It's likewise unknown why most histories of Spiritualism dismiss Phoebe with a cursory reference, giving pride of place to Kate and Maggie Fox, who in 1848 made contact with the spirit of a peddler murdered in their house. The sisters' turbulent story, skill at self-promotion, exploitation of Spiritualism as a road to social advancement, periods of poverty and prosperity, ups and downs, unhappy love affairs, humiliating body searches suffered before séances (meant to expose the instruments they used to produce "other-worldly" raps), battle against alcoholism, admission of fraud (the mysterious noises were created by cracking the big toe knuckle) only to renounce it later — all this has been the topic of innumerable books. No books have been penned on Phoebe, very likely because our knowledge of her lacks the human dimension. Of her tastes, friendships, addictions, we know almost nothing — and these are the things which interest readers of biographies. But maybe there's still time to reconstruct what for more than a hundred years researchers of Spiritualism have tried to erase.

IT HAS NOT YET SHOWN ITS TRUE COLOURS . . .

Phoebe's story seems to belong more to dream than reality, but everything in this town creates a similar impression. Even today, female inhabitants of the magic city of Providence are convinced Phoebe Hicks has been reborn in them. Bleached-blonde clerks, green-haired students in ripped jeans, the bored wives of bankers, are all united by a common secret : certainty that they are incarnations of the impostor medium. Her spirit soars over New England's provincial towns, mingles with the smell of fish and the ocean breeze. For reasons unknown, the guidebooks never mention her, a silence that smacks of conspiracy. Like a stubborn memory, the spirit of Phoebe Hicks tethers and smothers the lives of descendants of Atlantic fishermen, great-grandchildren of slave traders, new immigrants who settled not long ago, unaware of the dangers inherent in the place. It has not yet shown its true colours . . .

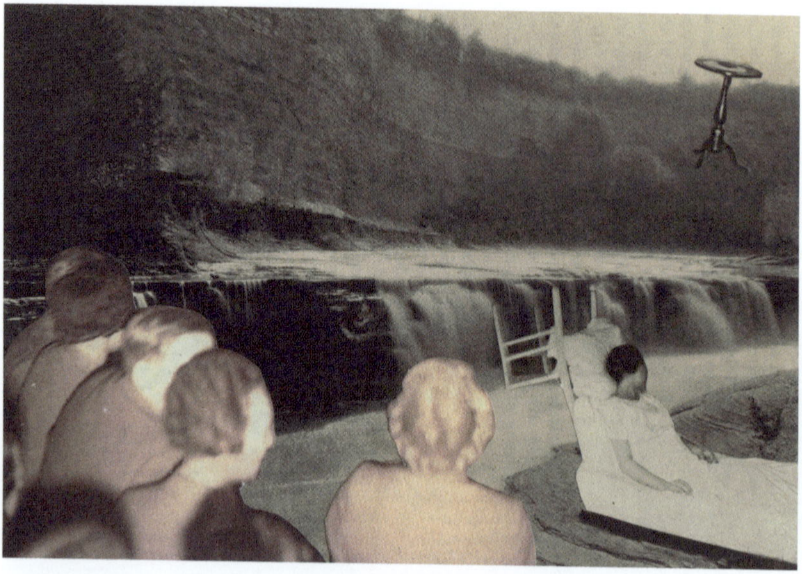

AGNIESZKA TABORSKA is a writer and art historian specializing in French Surrealism. She divides her time between Warsaw, Poland, and Providence, USA, where she teaches art history and literature at the Rhode Island School of Design. To date, she has published over twenty books in Polish, translated such authors as Spalding Gray, Roland Topor, Gisèle Prassinos, and Philippe Soupault into Polish, and has had translations of her work appear in English, French, German, Spanish, Slovak, Japanese, and Korean. Taborska has likewise curated exhibitions of Surrealist art in France and Poland, has written scripts for plays and documentary films related to Surrealism, and her two literary collaborations with visual artist Selena Kimball are experiments that reimagine Surrealism for the postmodern era.

SELENA KIMBALL is a visual artist who lives and works in Brooklyn, New York. While her emphasis is collage, she also works in painting, photography, and film and has exhibited in museums and galleries in the US, Mexico, France, Poland, and Romania. With Agnieszka Taborska she coauthored the collage novel, *The Dreaming Life of Leonora de la Cruz*, which has been published in Polish, English, Spanish, and French. She teaches at The New School's Parsons School of Design.

URSULA PHILLIPS writes on Polish literary history, and as a translator of literary and scholarly works has been instrumental in introducing to an Anglophone readership, both academic and general, Polish female authors from the 19th to 21st centuries, such as Narcyza Żmichowska's *The Heathen* (1846) and Zofia Nałkowska's *Choucas* (1927), for which she received the 2015 Found in Translation Award given by the Polish Book Institute, and *Boundary* (1935). Her translation of Jacek Dukaj's 1000-page alternative-history-cum-sci-fi epic *Ice* (2007) is published in 2024.

AGNIESZKA TABORSKA

THE UNFINISHED LIFE OF PHOEBE HICKS

with collages by Selena Kimball is translated by Ursula Phillips
from the original Polish *Niedokończone życie Phoebe Hicks*
(Gdańsk: Fundacja Terytoria Książki, 2013)

Layout and design by Silk Mountain

Set in Minion Pro

FIRST EDITION

Published in 2024 by
Twisted Spoon Press
P.O. Box 21 — Preslova 12
150 00 Prague 5
Czech Republic
www.twistedspoon.com

Printed and bound in the Czech Republic
by TISKÁRNA PROTISK, České Budějovice

TRADE DISTRIBUTION

CENTRAL BOOKS
www.centralbooks.com

SCB DISTRIBUTORS
www.scbdistributors.com